Signs of Rebirth

Signs of Rebirth

RUSSELL S. KANE

iUniverse, Inc.
Bloomington

Signs of Rebirth

iUniverse books may be ordered through booksellers or by contacting:

iUniverse
1663 Liberty Drive
Bloomington, IN 47403
www.iuniverse.com
1-800-Authors (1-800-288-4677)

ISBN: 978-1-4759-7870-4 (sc)
ISBN: 978-1-4759-7871-1 (ebk)

Library of Congress Control Number: 2013903618

Printed in the United States of America

iUniverse rev. date: 02/22/2013

Dedication

I would like to dedicate this second novel to my parents who have been a rock for me all these years. It is nice to see them learning ASL a little bit now. I also have some good friends who I want to recognize for their emotional support as I spent months and months writing this book: Jimmy Earle, Angela Tigner, Rooshanak Salimi, Ritwik Routh, Linda Krongold. My colleagues in the communications department at Nassau Community College have been terrific, asking me how my novel was coming along. I am also extremely lucky to have so many wonderful ASL students at NCC. It would take me so many pages to list all of those who gave me such positive feedback on my first novel, _Fighting the Long Sorrow_. Last, but not least, HAND-WAVE to all of my Facebook friends who kept asking me when this second novel was coming out. Thank you all for your continued support and please spread the word about my books. I am currently working on my third which should be coming out next year in 2014.

Chapter 1

Lindsay Veniglio was really nervous as she looked at the computer screen for Las Vegas Community College's website. It was her first time signing up for ASL classes. She had been captivated with ASL ever since she found a Helen Keller book at her public library at the urging of her third-grade teacher, Mrs. Conway. She was supposed to do a project on a woman that had a profound impact on American history. She had walked into the library ready to burst into tears, as she had no idea who to do the poster about, but thanks to the librarian at the desk, she was given Helen Keller's name.

Getting an "A+" on her poster, she continued to read about and research on Helen Keller throughout her elementary and high school years. Now she was a self-proclaimed scholar on Keller and even had taught herself the alphabet that deaf people used. Now that she was done with high school, she felt ready to take the next step and enroll in ASL classes for credit at the college level. Sadly, her high school had not offered any ASL classes so she had to wait until now.

Lindsay was what you would call a "looker". She was of average height, but her beauty was very evident. She was a full-blooded Italian, with black hair that curled to her shoulders. She had big brown eyes and a svelte physique. Many guys had fallen for her in high school, but she had never dated anyone. They were all immature to her. She wanted to wait for the college boys and here she was! She had never been so happy to see a graduation day in her life and she was more than ready for LVCC. Who would she meet? She had often wondered about this after-high school experience. She would find out soon enough.

Her eyes roamed all over the LVCC website, looking for anything about registration. On the left side, she read down until she came across "Online Registration" and her hand slapped the desk. That was it! Moving the mouse, she clicked on the link. Eventually, she found a list of classes and scrolled down the list of classes for ASL 101. She saw that there was an 8 a.m. to 9:30 a.m. class on Mondays and Wednesdays. That was perfect! Some guy named Reggie Kelleher was teaching it. Who was this Kelleher guy? She researched the faculty of the ASL program and saw that there were two teachers who were full-time and doing the day classes: Kelleher and some woman named Sara Zaslow who was probably hearing, as she got her degrees from hearing colleges including one in audiology and speech therapy.

She had no idea who the teachers were, but she had been told that it was better to have a deaf teacher rather than a hearing teacher because of the cultural aspect. It did make sense because she wanted a professor who had grown up deaf and knew the struggles of dealing with hearing people every day. She had an idea and opened up a new tab page with Google, then typed in "Reggie Kelleher" in the search bar. Ah, he was deaf and had gone to Gallaudet University for both his BA and MA degrees! That was pure gold.

The decision was made. She proceeded to click on the class and registered for it. There were not many seats left. The class limit was only 22? That was really strange because all of her other classes had a limit of 30 or more students. Was there some reason for this smaller number? She figured she would find out soon enough, as the class started next week. She was very happy to have found an actual deaf teacher. She navigated her way back to the ASL page at LVCC and confirmed that there were two professors teaching ASL there for the day classes. One was deaf and one was hearing. She did not want to take night classes, as she felt nervous walking around the campus after dark. Now she felt even luckier having found this Kelleher's class. She logged off and decided to drive the ten minutes to the college's bookstore to buy the books for her classes.

The price of these books was ridiculous, she thought. Whoever heard of $100 for one book for one class? To her, it was highway robbery! LVCC was only a few minutes drive from her parents' house. There were no dorms there, as it was a two-year college. There were not too many people there, as classes were starting next week. With her left hand gripping the schedule, she walked into the bookstore. She looked around the inside of the small building and her eyes saw that the books were placed by department. The bookstore was not even big enough to hold all of the books carried by LVCC. Some were even in the middle of the floor stacked in piles. There were only a few people inside. She also saw lockers just outside the entrance, in the lobby. They were strict about security here, not allowing anyone to bring books inside. This was in response to the recent thefts that she had read about in the newspaper.

ASL was one of the first from the left so that was easy to find. She saw a few other women standing around near the ASL books so she scanned the course names for ASL 101. Interestingly, all of the books were the same for ASL 101, no matter which teacher was listed. She saw the names Kelleher and Zaslow. This was definitely the right place. Out of curiosity, she looked at the books for ASL 102 which she planned to take in the spring. The same workbook, <u>*Signing Naturally*</u>, was there. That would save her and the other students some money!

Only three books? That was not bad! <u>*Deaf Again*</u> by Mark Drolsbaugh, <u>*Fighting the Long Sorrow*</u> by Russell Kane, and <u>*Signing Naturally*</u> were the three required texts for these ASL 101 classes. She had never even heard of those two male authors. Were they deaf? She picked up the two books, turned them over, and nodded. Yup, they were both deaf and Gallaudet graduates! This was turning out to be even better.

The prices were not too bad, $16 or so for each book. Uh-oh, that <u>*Signing Naturally*</u> looked expensive to her. There were two DVDs in the back, sealed in a plastic cover. She was afraid to take a peek on the back cover, but she had no choice. Seventy dollars for a single book?!?! Her eyes wandered over to the books for ASL 102 again to make sure that the same workbook was required for that class. Now, $70 did not seem so bad to her anymore.

"Prepare yourself for sticker shock!" That voice came from behind her. Must be one of the other women standing there. She put the book down and turned around. Yes, it was one of the women standing around the ASL book section.

"Really? How bad is it?" She really was curious. Ah, it was the woman wearing a polka-dot dress, all flowery and high heels. She was very tall and appeared to be debonair. She had a gorgeous face with two dimples, one on each cheek. She had sunglasses resting on her blonde hair which was pulled back. What was this, the deep South debutante ball? This woman looked totally out of place here. Lindsay wanted to be nice and not judge a book by its cover.

"What is your name, by the way? Mine is Lindsay Veniglio, enrolled in ASL 101 with Reggie Kelleher."

Polka-Dot Dress laughed and exclaimed, "You have Rego? Oh, poor you! My name is Kimberly Davidson. Friends call me Kimmie." Her eyes opened in sympathy for this clueless student who was about to get the shock of her life in Rego's class. Everyone found out sooner or later about Rego's inflated self-worth and swelled head. He was impossible to please and the stricter of the two ASL professors.

Rego was so picky about everything, from what Kimmie had heard. Also, he preferred students to post their assignments on Turnitin.com so he would not have to lug papers around. He was notorious for giving almost no feedback on their work. God forbid she take any classes with Rego! As in never.

"Who is Rego? My schedule says Kelleher. Was there a typo in there?" Lindsay was confused. Her forehead crinkled in consternation. What did Kimmie know that she didn't? All of a sudden, she felt inadequate and stupid for not knowing who this Rego was right off the bat.

"My bad. Rego is our nickname for Kelleher. He is such a pompous ass, excuse my language. We call him Rego because he has the biggest ego on the campus, perhaps in the entire world! Reggie we turned into the sign name for A-T-T-I-T-U-D-E as thus (counterclockwise "A" with right hand on left chest) so we use 'R' in place of that." Thus, sign name R-E-G-O!" She finished the sign with a flourish. The other two women standing with Kimmie nodded enthusiastically. "The three of us have Professor Sara Zaslow who is very easy and boring—she has a flat personality, but she passes everyone if you buy her a cup of java! We call her Professor Z, as she puts us to sleep! We survived Kelleher so you can, too!"

Lindsay felt totally out of her element. These women signed so well and classes had not even started. How was that possible? Was she going to be so far behind on the first day? "Umm . . . are you guys in 101 or 102?" Crossing her fingers, she awaited Kimmie's answer.

"Oh, we are in 102!" Kimmie laughed and looked at her friends. "We had Rego last semester . . ." She giggled at the mere utterance of his derogatory nickname. She composed herself and continued, "It was a mess! The whole class wrote a letter of protest to the chair, the dean, and the president about Rego's teaching style. Of course, nothing happened. He is tenured."

Uh-oh. Ego? As in Rego? That didn't sound so good to Lindsay. Was it too late to change classes to this Zaslow? Impossible. The only 101 teacher was Kelleher, so she had to make do with what she had. No, she vowed to stick with the deaf professor, no matter what. She knew that tough professors had high standards and pushed students to meet them. "Is this Rego as bad as you say he is? What kind of things are you talking about with him?"

Kimmie sighed and her head tilted back. "From the stories I've heard about him, he puts students down in class, is condescending, always talks about himself, thinks he's the funniest guy on the planet, and doesn't allow anyone in after attendance no matter what happens. He demands that you read everything multiple times for his tough final exam that is one hundred questions long at the end of the semester. Nobody ever passes that test. He had to curve it 20 points, as nobody got an A or a B. Isn't that ridiculous?" She looked at the other two women who nodded. There was no way she was going to take Rego's class ever again. Let Lindsay find out for herself. "The class we are in is full and so are all of Z's other classes. Good luck to you! By the way, the Signing Naturally is $70, but you use it for ASL 101 and 102 here so that's not too bad."

Oh, well. $70 divided by two was $35.00 so that was somewhat more palatable to her. She had been right in thinking this workbook was for two full semesters of ASL. Lindsay was worried though about taking Rego. Maybe she could postpone to the spring semester in hopes that Rego would be elsewhere? No! She became more determined to thrive in Rego's class no matter what he threw at her. She wanted to become fluent in ASL.

Plus, Rego had to have some redeeming qualities, right? It could not be all bad! She grabbed the cleanest looking copy of *Signing Naturally* she could find, plus *Deaf Again* and *Fighting the Longest Sorrow*. Before she left Kimmie, she eyed this Southern belle again and her two friends. They looked a lot like her with similar-looking dresses and expensive handbags. What was it with these Jersey Shore wannabes? Didn't they have a mind of their own? She marched off to the cash register after getting all of the other books for her two other classes. Paying by credit card, she hurried out of the bookstore, as she could not wait to separate herself from those three negative women as quickly as possible.

Chapter 2

Little did Reggie Kelleher have any clue this semester was going to be drastically different from any other semester at LVCC. Driving to school the first day of classes for the fall semester of 2011, he hummed while parking in the faculty lot right in front of his office building, Smithson Hall. It was still early in the morning with plenty of time to spare until the 8:00 a.m. ASL class which was the first one of the day. Reggie sat in his 2001 Honda Civic LX with its gray interior. He had grown to love the car which never had broken down over the past ten years since he bought it brand-new.

He felt very lucky to live in Las Vegas, the gambling capital of the world. He had grown up in a suburb near the Strip and he became very familiar with the hustle and bustle with the traffic and businesses as a teenager. His childhood had been somewhat mundane, as his mother was a homemaker and his father was a prominent businessman who had dealings with the casinos and hotels. Reggie had a few favorites on the Strip growing up and cherished the history of the older casinos on the northern part of the Strip. Anytime there was a special on TV about the Rat Pack or any celebrities frequenting these older casinos, he was sure to be glued to the boob tube.

His dad had been an amazing businessman. The only person Reggie could think of who held a candle to his dad was Donald

Trump. Unless you were on Mars over the past few decades, you (and five billion others) knew who Maxwell Joshua Kelleher was. Anytime he ran into someone new and mentioned his last name, the first reaction usually was, "Hey, are you related to the Maxwell Joshua Kelleher that I've seen on the news?" Reggie always nodded and gave his pat answer: "Yes, that's my father and I am very proud of him! My name is Reggie."

For some reason, his dad always insisted on using all three names, but people always told him it sounded like some presidential would-be assassin or certifiably insane asylum resident. Think about it. Lee Harvey Oswald, John Wilkes Booth, John Wayne Gacy. Not exactly the most esteemed company! But, whatever, he still loved his dad. But he had not always felt that way, as his dad had always been away on business, taking care of a megamillion dollar deal here and there due to the nature of his gambling ties. What was even more amazing about this story is that Reggie was profoundly deaf, yet his dad had never felt sorry for him. He was even more like Trump who pushed his four kids to success.

Continuing to sit in his Honda, Reggie thought about how he had been born deaf in both ears due to unknown causes. After the 1960's, there was a considerable drop in the number of deaf babies due to the rubella vaccination. He was born in 1974. His dad was a fluent signer and so was his mother. Why was that? When he was diagnosed deaf, his parents threw themselves into ASL classes, learning about Deaf culture and learning all about ASL linguistics.

One of the most profound books he had ever come across was Paddy Ladd's outstanding opus, _Understanding Deaf Culture: In Search of Deafhood_. This book was still available online and through catalogs. Reggie knew from his graduate studies that deafhood was not a biological term. It was more of the overall process of accepting one's deafness in a positive way. Ever since the 2006 Gallaudet protest over the appointment of Jane K. Fernandes as the new president, which ended up in her resignation, Deafhood became a very well-known term in the Deaf community. Any research that some did about Deafhood always started with Ladd's book. There also was a Facebook page dedicated solely to Deafhood so that was another excellent place to start.

Reggie also had been recently exposed to two excellent books that he now used in his classes at LVCC: *Fighting the Long Sorrow* by Russell Kane, an ASL professor at Nassau Community College, and *Deaf Again* by Mark Drolsbaugh. Both were really interesting reads and he got many positive reviews from his students at the end of each semester on both. Drolsbaugh also had written several other books which Reggie always recommended to his classes. He knew that Kane was just finishing up his second and was in the process of editing it with the publisher before it came out.

Growing up, Reggie had never had siblings. This way, he had his parents' full attention with using ASL and it had opened doors for him to chat with his grandparents, aunts, uncles, cousins and everyone who knew his parents. He had always enjoyed the family reunions with his parents taking turns interpreting. All of his relatives spoke slowly to him and whenever he was in their presence, they made sure he was included. He did feel very lucky.

His dad had explained to him how casinos really operated along with the hotels on the Strip. While most boys at sixteen were obsessed with video games, girls, and cars, he was already learning the ins and outs of Vegas establishments.

By the time Reggie graduated from high school, he could pretty much give an exhaustive tour of the Strip and tell you which hotels were the better ones and even give you the names/titles of every hotel's manager along with which had the better odds for betting on a specific kind of parlor game. He was an expert in doing over-unders (predicting total of two team's scores in a game) in any sports game, whether at the professional or college level. When he was with his dad at betting places, there was always a lot of noise, but that never had bothered him because of his deafness.

By the time he was ready for Gallaudet University, he was a self-made millionaire from buying stock in establishments that his dad worked with. It was one step away from getting insider information about stocks, but it was all legal. He knew which companies were efficiently run. He also could analyze which stocks were extremely weak so he had shorted them, betting that they would not do well. He profited handsomely with long and short stocks. Two major purchases that had done well for him were Apple and Netflix. He had a feeling that Apple would plumment within the next twelve months with the products not being innovative enough. He was planning to short that stock soon. He also had bought eBay, Chipotle, and a few others that quadrupled or more in a very short time.

He chuckled thinking about his mom. She was a pillar of strength, as she became an ASL freelance interpreter even though she was mainly a homemaker when he was growing up. After he flew the coop and became an adult, she had gone back to school and recently got her certification. She was one of the most prominent leaders in the Deaf community. She was one of those who had pushed for the upgrading of standards for educational interpreters to have a BA degree for certification.

He marveled at the circumstances that brought him to LVCC. He had gone to a happy hour event a few years ago and had been unaware of the existence of the Deaf Studies program at LVCC.

One woman he signed with at the event mentioned it to him and gave him Sara Zaslow's name and email information. He had been intrigued and wrote to her. One thing led to another and here he was. The LVCC campus was pretty new, as it had been built to accommodate the incredibly fast-growing population growth of Las Vegas' suburbs during the 1990's and beyond. That was one of the advantages of working at a new community college with everything so modern.

How many classes did he have? Seven again! All full-time professors had a courseload of five three-credit classes so that semester, he had five ASL 101 sections plus two more for adjunct pay. The salary at LVCC was pathetically low around $35,000 a year for a full-time instructor so the adjunct classes were absolutely a lifesaver for a bachelor like him, paying $3,000 each. That was a fortune with Vegas' low cost of living.

Reggie Kelleher, a bachelor? Technically not, as he had a girlfriend who was pretty demanding in that she required that he pay for all of their dates. He personally thought it was ridiculous in this day and age. If it were the 1950's, with women staying home and cooking/cleaning, that would be fine with him. Now, with women's lib, why should men be paying for the engagement ring, dates, etc.? Don't get him started on the happy hour when women got in for free and men had to pay $10 just for the privilege of stepping into a bar!

It really wasn't that bad. He had gotten lucky and was teaching only ASL 101 that semester. His office mate and ASL teaching colleague, Sara Zaslow, preferred to teach ASL 102, for some reason, so she had arranged it so that she had two sections of 102, giving adjuncts the rest of the courseload. She was also the lab coordinator so that made up for the remaining three classes in a typical courseload.

Reggie knew that Sara Zaslow was a very efficient, yet boring person. She dressed the same every day, black pants and jacket with a white shirt every day. Was it because she used to be a nun? Who knows? She was beautiful, though. She had long hair and high cheekbones with olive skin. He had to admit that he was very attracted to her physically, but for some reason he thought she would never want to consider him as more than a friend and colleague. He could imagine Sara all dressed up with makeup and jewelry. He had no doubt that all eyes would be on her if she ever went that route.

All he knew was that Sara was a devout Christian who had been the ultimate Catholic until something happened in her convent. Nobody knew what it was, but it had driven her out of the profession into the secular world. He could remember one discussion they had about her beliefs including the Rapture, Tribulation, and Judgment Day. She had even lent him a copy of the Alberto comic books which had led her to the Pentecostals. They also had many discussions about the pedophilia scandal that rocked the Catholic Church over the past few years. This did contribute to Sara's leaving the Church eventually.

Upon arrival at the department office, he checked his mailbox and saw there were rosters waiting for him. Oh, joy! Time to find out who his students were. He did a quick scan of the names and of course over ninety percent of the names were female. That was typical of ASL classes throughout his years at LVCC. Why was that, though? Was it because women are more prevalent in the helping professions than men? Or was it that women had a more open heart for others? Interestingly enough, most of the men who became ASL fluent were gay themselves so he felt sorry for any guy who was in his ASL classes. Approximately 75% of men dropped out due to their not keeping up with the work and being absent from his classes.

He chuckled at a story that he often shared with colleagues and friends. At a party, years ago, he had run into a brand-new student of ASL who was attending Dutchess Community College in upstate New York. This student, Greg, was in Las Vegas on vacation and was at a workshop that he was at also. They had been standing near the stage, watching a show by some comedian in a ridiculous-looking costume, red cape and all. He had no interest in watching and happened to start a conversation with this Greg.

It turned out Greg was just starting to learn ASL and Reggie had actually felt sorry for him! He told Greg that gay men tended to do very well while straight men usually struggled and it would be a tough road for him on the way to ASL fluency. The edges of Greg's mouth curled up as he told Reggie he was gay. Reggie had felt like he had a shoe in his mouth! Sure enough, he heard years later that Greg became a certified interpreter, confirming his gay interpreter theory yet again.

Was there something in the female DNA that gave them the better aptitude for learning ASL? Their hands were more capable of handling the four parameters: handshape, location, palm orientation, and movement. This was something he emphasized in ASL 101 with students as a way of analyzing signs that appeared similar. For example, two signs—BLACK and SUMMER—were often confused in class by students until he explained to them on the blackboard that there was a difference in handshape with these two words—BLACK saw the index finger remain the same at "1" while SUMMER had the index finger change from "1" to "x". Students never forgot that ever again. It showed up as a question on many quizzes at LVCC and students often got it wrong because they just did not study for a pop quiz.

With the rosters in his right hand, he hurried to his office that he shared with Sara. It was really interesting to see her voice with signing-impaired (a.k.a. hearing people who do not sign—a piece of deaf humor here) professors when he was in the same room. Normally, with deaf etiquette, anyone who can sign should be signing whenever a deaf person is in the same room, but he had consulted with Sara before about that. He told her previously that there was no need to sign even with him there because it would confuse the other hearing professors in the department. It was one of the many adjustments they had made as officemates at LVCC. They agreed that once the non-signer was out of the office, she would summarize a conversation for him if it was related to their ASL program.

On a side note—LVCC's deaf studies classes used the "Sign of Respect" DVD made by Tom Holcomb which emphasized what is important in Deaf culture with etiquette and customs. One of the major points was that a hearing person was not expected to interpret a conversation on the phone or in person if there was a deaf bystander nearby unless the hearing person was fluent in ASL. Then, the expectations changed. This was a favorite trick question on Reggie's final exam which was one hundred questions long, all multiple-choice. He liked seeing his students being challenged and tested to see if they really studied.

Getting that out of his mind, he spied his class bag behind his desk and smiled. It was a good thing he had prepared the week before for this first day of classes. It was always nice to not have to hurry at the last minute. He made sure he had his teacher's edition of *Signing Naturally* along with *Deaf Again* and *Fighting the Long Sorrow* in his bag.

He was lucky enough to have met Mark Drolsbaugh and Russell Kane when he went to visit some friends who lived on Long

Island. He had never heard of NCC's ASL program before coming. He had been at a friend's house and saw a posting on Facebook for a lecture series by Drolsbaugh and Kane about their books so he called up the Student Activities Club through video relay service to make sure he could come during the day. They told him yes so he had parked in that huge parking lot "A" at NCC near the campus security trailer and ran into Drolsbaugh and Kane just outside Building CCB before the workshop had started. They got to talking about their experiences and that was when Reggie realized how truly lucky he was.

Drolsbaugh had deaf parents, but they refused to allow him to sign. Kane had hearing parents who did not give him exposure to ASL so he, like Drolsbaugh, had to wait until he was in his twenties before learning at Gallaudet like Drolsbaugh did. However, both had been very lucky to have supportive and attentive parents that pushed them with education, literacy, and being able to communicate in the hearing world. Reggie had hearing parents who were fluent in ASL because they took classes and practiced in the Deaf community. He always had felt welcome at family events with them interpreting for him anytime he needed communication access. Kane did tell him that his parents were now learning ASL and that he was very excited about that prospect.

After talking with the two men, he had bought Drolsbaugh's and Kane's books, enjoyed them tremendously, and decided to use them in ASL 101 with Sara's agreement. It was the beginning of a friendship with them on Facebook. Kane recently told him that his book hit the top 100 on Amazon's Kindle for American dramatic fiction which was a huge accomplishment. He often wondered why Gallaudet did not promote this book, as it was the only novel in the world that covered Deaf President Now, an important and pivotal movement that changed Gallaudet itself forever and the

Deaf world should be aware of this novel's existence. It was almost twenty-five years since DPN had happened, so he would have imagined that Gallaudet would promote Kane's book as part of that.

What time was it? 7:45 a.m. Time to go to the first class that started at 8 a.m. in Smithson Hall—it was really nice having classes and an office in the same building. Just a few steps between the two places really made a difference, as students often came after class to talk to him about various issues. Reggie was really nervous, as he always was at the beginning of each semester. He never slept well the night before classes started again. He had tossed and turned, looking at his alarm every hour or two. It really bothered him that this always happened, but it was just one or two nights then he was fine after that.

He always felt that the previous semester was the best one and he would not have such great classes again, but he was proven wrong every time. Taking a deep breath, he opened the door to his classroom, not knowing this would be the most important class of his entire life.

Entering the room, he saw students sitting all around the room in rows. He smiled to himself like he did every semester for the first class session. These students had no idea what was going to hit them in a few minutes! Deaf culture was something best taught by experience. It was one thing to read it in a book or be told about it by someone, but to see it first-hand was really something else. On with the show! He walked over to the desk that he had seen for a few semesters already. Same desk, same chair, same overhead. This room he had used already and it was a good size for the number of students they usually had, which was 22.

His college, for whatever reason, had increased the cap on the class size from 16 to 22 due to Nevada's serious budget issues and

LVCC being in the deep red. Sara and he had tried appealing to the board of trustees and to President Barron to no avail. They just did not understand how ASL classes worked so they were stuck with having 22 students. But that would not be a problem for long due to the attendance policy that Sara and he had maintained as part of their ASL classes. It was college policy to allow three absences then they had the right as professors to withdraw a student upon the fourth absence according to the college catalog and their syllabi. It usually took a few weeks to bring the class size down to approximately 15 so that was something to wait for.

In the meantime, students suffered in the classrooms that were way too small for the purpose of teaching ASL. What hearing administrators did not understand was that classes were held with desks in a semicircle which took up a lot of space. They did the best they could. It was just slow going for the first month and the pace sped up as the class size diminished, allowing classes to cover more material in a shorter amount of time.

Chapter 3

Lindsay was so nervous she was in danger of hyperventilating. She was seated up front on the far side of the room near the radiator and windows. She had no idea what to expect and braced herself for the worst. Her encounter with Kimmie had not helped at all. She took another look at the textbooks she bought and steeled herself for anything. She really wanted to become fluent in ASL, come hell or high water. She wanted to have a career using ASL and there was no place to start better than now with a deaf teacher.

She looked around the room at the other students. Some were chatting with each other openly. They were sitting in random desks and she knew they had no idea about the semicircle that Professor Kelleher would be asking them to sit in. The only reason she knew was because she had learned it from Kimmie in the bookstore. So, when she seated herself, she had her back to the window and was facing the door. She was the only one who obviously knew what was coming with the seating arrangements. All of the other students had looked at her strangely as if there was something wrong with her. She ignored them and awaited Kelleher's arrival which should be any minute. She knew he was very punctual and often early.

LVCC was a good college with a lot of support in place for its students and alumni. She was going to do it! The room was very quiet once Kelleher walked in with his books and papers. Even though people knew this professor was deaf and they could get away with voicing, nobody dared risk it. Everyone had heard of Kelleher's legendary temper, flaring at whoever was caught breaking the no-voicing rule which was sacrosanct in an ASL class. They knew he had thrown out students for the slightest offense which included voicing and checking cell phones. He had also seized assignments that were done wrong in terms of format and ripped them up. He was a real tyrant!

Taking a look at Mr. Kelleher, she did a momentary overview of what he appeared to be like. His hair was so short! She never liked long hair and could not understand the appeal of some women to guys like that character in "Hunger Games" . . . what was his name? Mitch Abernathy. Some women actually liked that. Not her. Guys with long hair seemed so unkempt and out of place teaching in a classroom, no matter what age the students were. It ruined, at least for her, the overall impression of a professor.

Kelleher was dressed in a polo shirt, solid red. He had beige slacks on, flat in the front. At least they were not pleated! That drove her crazy because it was so out of style. She had had teachers in high school with pleated slacks and it bothered her. Those shoes he was wearing were questionable. Were they really shoes or sneakers? At least the shoes were not white! Even his socks were black which was a good thing. If they had been white, she would have felt like screaming, "Nerd alert!"

Overall, he was not a bad looking guy. He was of average height. Maybe a little taller than she had expected. Glasses. No hearing aids? She thought all deaf people wore some kind of hearing aid. What about a cochlear implant? Nope. Not this teacher. Looks like he may be hard of hearing unless he just could not hear a single thing. She did not want to be too obvious so she watched him as he wrote on the blackboard. Still could not see anything behind the ears.

What was he writing? She craned her neck and saw it as he moved away. "Sit in a semicircle"? She chuckled and felt good that she had been proven right. The other students who had looked at her strangely before gave her dirty looks. Never before had she ever seen that in a class in her life! It did make sense. If ASL was all visual, everyone was going to have to be able to see each other. She stayed where she was and saw that everyone else was moving their desk into a semicircle facing the blackboard. She noticed Kelleher watching with amusement. Was that a slight smirk on his face? He did not seem too nice to be watching like that, arms folded, right foot tapping the floor slightly as if he were bored already.

As Kelleher walked over back to the desk, she saw "ASL 101—Professor Reggie Kelleher" on the board and was relieved she was in the right class. This college was huge and it was easy to get lost on campus too easily. More people sauntered in just before 8 a.m. and then she heard a tapping. What was that? Kelleher was knocking the desk! Why didn't he just shout for attention? Duh, this was an ASL class.

Everyone stopped typing on their smart phones and put them on their desks. Kelleher shook his head and pointed at each smart phone he saw. His face was one of obvious displeasure. She knew that if he saw them with a cell phone after today, they would be booted from class before they even knew it. Obviously he wanted them to put them away. She knew that this was a pet peeve of professors at this college, seeing students with smart phones on their desks. She couldn't blame him for feeling that way.

She did a head count of the class. There were now twenty students in the room including her. Two were missing. She knew this class had been full as of yesterday so two more were unaccounted for. Her eyes stayed riveted on Kelleher as he wrote his name on the board: REGGIE. He turned around back to the class and did something with his right hand. Fingerspelling! Her favorite activity since she was a little girl in third grade learning about Helen Keller. She caught the letters one by one, mouthing as he spelled his name. Suddenly, she found him standing near her, head shaking. He made a motion of zipping his lips. Oops, she had not realized she was mouthing each letter. She smiled nervously and nodded.

He walked backwards to the desk and pointed to REGGIE, then pointed to himself. Obviously, it was his name. She copied as he fingerspelled it again. Everyone else was doing the same thing. So far, so good! Then, he picked up a piece of paper and made another motion. Ah, PAPER. Two palms out facing each other, kind of like clapping, but a bit different. More of a passing movement. She took out a piece of paper and a pen. Kelleher pointed to REGGIE and signed with both hands, using his index and middle fingers out. That must mean NAME. He pointed to himself and then NAME. Pointed to REGGIE. Yes!

Each student walked up to the board and wrote his or her name. Then, he or she struggled as Kelleher showed him or her how to spell his or her name. That took approximately twenty minutes. Then, it was suddenly her turn, as she was the last one left. Gulping, she forced herself to get up and go over to the board to write her name: LINDSAY. She faced Kelleher and fingerspelled it quickly without any help. His eyebrows arched up in surprise. Now she had impressed him! An auspicious start to the semester!

But he wrote on the blackboard: "Faster is not better when fingerspelling. Be controlled, do not bounce your hand, go medium speed." She nodded as Kelleher pointed to what he had written. Boy, was he picky. She spelled her name again and this time he approved. Whew. She had made it through with nineteen other students watching every move she made. She hurried back to her desk and sat down quickly. Kelleher then took out some sheets and motioned for students to pass them along. A quiz already? Her pulse quickened as she took the sheets and passed them along, keeping one for herself. True or False Pre-Test! This should be interesting. She glanced at all ten statements and had no idea about some of them. She saw Kelleher motion for them to circle for each statement.

All twenty heads faced the desks as they read the statements. Kelleher walked around the room checking on their progress. Some of these were tough to guess. Do deaf people read Braille? Heck, no. She laughed at that one. Only blind people do. At least she knew that much! Does ASL have the same grammatical rules as English? Of course it did. That would make sense. She circled TRUE or FALSE for each sentence and when the class proceeded to go through the pre-test with Kelleher, she was surprised that ASL and English did not have the same rules at all. She looked at the other students who had the same facial expression of surprise registered. Kelleher kept her and the others on their toes with statistics that she hurried to write down, as she knew these would be on the infamous final exam, such as:

> 90% of deaf children have hearing parents
> The average deaf HS graduate has a fourth grade reading level
> Deaf people are better drivers than hearing people

Only 30% of what is uttered is visible on the lips

60% of deaf people are unemployed

The information was eye-opening and Lindsay was happy that she was in this class. She doubted that Zaslow's class covered this amount of material. Hearing the knock, she looked at Kelleher who was pointing to his watch. Time was up already? She really liked this class and had learned a lot in just an hour and half. Kelleher was packing up his bag when she went up to him and signed THANK-YOU to him. That really surprised him, as she could see from his facial expression. But he still did not smile. She turned around and walked out of the classroom. Did Kelleher ever smile? She doubted it.

As she exited the classroom, a gaggle of students was standing outside in the hallway chattering about the class that had just ended. She could hear bits and pieces, but nothing seemed interesting until she heard, "Let's continue the traditional pool going to bet on when Rego first smiles this semester! How about it?" They all became excited and she saw five dollar bills being handed over to one student who was obviously the ringleader of the group. She was intrigued so she walked over and wedged her way into the group which numbered seven students.

"Hi, my name is Lindsay Veniglio—I couldn't help overhearing there is a pool going. Count me in! Seeing this is Las Vegas, why not bet on something fun like this!" The others laughed and one even slapped her on the back. She rummaged through her purse and came up with a five-dollar bill. With a pen, she wrote "The class before Thanksgiving!" She plucked it out as if she were a magician and pointed the bill to the student who was taking money from everyone else. "What's your name? Just so I know I am not just forking over my hard-earned dough to a stranger!" She smiled as she finished saying that so that everyone would know she was just teasing.

It obviously worked as the other woman laughed in return, eyes fixed on Lindsay. "That is a good one! My name is Sally Seacreti and all of us went to high school together so that's why we already are acquainted here. You are welcome to participate in the pool. Let's see when Rego first smiles!"

Lindsay nodded vigorously as Sally kept talking. She wasn't really paying attention, as everyone else was trying to talk over her. It was proving to be very confusing right there, but she got the gist of what Sally was trying to say about the origin of Rego's nickname. Luckily, she had learned about it in the bookstore.

"Are you serious that Reggie . . . I mean, Rego . . ." It was strange to be saying that nickname to refer to her own ASL teacher. "He has a really big ego, that big?" She was incredulous. How could he keep his job with a negative attitude like that?

Another student in the group chimed in. "You better believe it! My friend who is deaf knows Rego from when she was growing up. She even talked about him when we were in high school. I dreaded the day I would walk into his classroom at LVCC and now here we are, surviving the first day of the semester with him! Hi, Lindsay. My name is Tabitha Johnson, but you can call me Tabby or even Tab like everyone else does. I don't want to sound like the witch on TV!"

Lindsay laughed and immediately liked this group. Suddenly, everyone quieted down and faces turned to the door of the classroom. Rego came out with a scowl on his face. Another girl in the group exclaimed, "Oh damn it! I just lost the pool! I figured he would smile hello when he left the classroom today and then win the entire money pile in a minute." Her head hung as she finished her sentence. Everyone's eyes were riveted on Rego's every move as he stared down the group while walking to the double doors. Like a cowboy, Rego pushed the door open and strolled down the stairs as if he were the sheriff of town. Sighs emanated from the girls in the group as they all pondered on their fate being in this class for sixteen weeks.

Was Rego going to be this bad? She wondered if the rumors had a grain of truth in them. Two months went by very quickly and Lindsay had promised herself that she would go to a lot of deaf events to practice her ASL. Unknowst to her classmates, she made many deaf friends and really expanded her vocabulary to the point where she knew more ASL than even the ASL 4 students. It was all a matter of immersion. She never forgot the story that Reggie told the class about the two Gallaudet hearing women who dated deaf guys from August to November and became fluent as a result. That had made a huge impact on her.

Chapter 4

Sheesh, what was wrong with these giggly girls? Reggie could not understand why students wanted to take ASL and then suddenly discard it the minute they stepped out of a classroom. Didn't they ever hear of showing respect for ASL by not voicing right outside his own classroom? What was wrong with this generation? Everyone had a cell phone on the desk and he sensed an aura of entitlement among these kids, as their high schools probably let them use cell phones during school hours. Now they were whispering among each other. Even though he was bad with names, he remembered Lindsay and Sally already. They were going to be trouble this semester. He did not like the way they were staring at him as he walked past them.

Wait, why was Lindsay holding some five-dollar bills in her hand? Was she collecting bets on something? This was Vegas and anything was possible. Shaking his head and giving the students the evil eye, he pushed the double doors open as if he were Wyatt Earp to show them who was the real leader in town. There was no room for anyone usurping him nor disrespecting ASL by voicing right outside his door. That was the norm here, as he had taught at LVCC for a few years. Technically, they were not breaking any rules as they had already stepped outside his classroom.

Reggie did not really care. He had to go home to a girlfriend who was becoming more bossy by the day. Why was he staying with her anyway? Sighing, he sauntered down the steps slowly, not wanting to slip and fall in front of students. Finally arriving on the first floor, he felt more steady on his feet without those beady eyes watching his every move. Sighing, he shook his head at their audacity in voicing right in front of him.

Why were they taking ASL classes anyway? He worked at LVCC for the fun of teaching itself. Who needed their patronizing attitude in class and out? All of his coworkers were hearing and he wondered what it would be like to work at Gallaudet surrounded by many deaf colleagues along with hearing ones who signed. He probably would never find out, as he had tenure here and didn't want the risk of starting over somewhere else.

Classes came and went. The weeks and months blurred into each other and time went by quickly. For some reason, the following classes did not impact him as much as the first one did early that first morning. He did not see any more students voicing in the hallway, exchanging five dollar bills, watching him walk away as if they were SWAT sharpshooters. It was always a relief to head home.

He actually lived across the street in some house that was owned by a private realty company—they had some ties to the college and he had been lucky to snatch up a house rental for a really good price. His father had a lot of connections and he knew some were alliances with the Mob. He could remember verbatim what his dad told him when he was in fifth grade, all curious about the Mafia. Dad loved to call it Nostre Familia and it was their code when Dad explained it all to him. Over the years, he abbreviated the fingerspelling to "N-F" whenever he saw anyone even faintly resembling a mafioso near them. It was for the family's own safety.

He knew Dad had not exactly been a saint when he was younger, in his real estate dealings.

Reggie could already have had a Ph.D. in Las Vegas history. Many people did not know that Vegas was "discovered" in 1829 by a Mexican scout barely out of his teens. He had been looking for a trade route from Santa Fe, New Mexico, to Los Angeles, California. He realized that Vegas' location was perfect with abundant wild grasses and an ample water supply. Traders could stop and rest during the long, hard journey from Santa Fe to Los Angeles. "Las Vegas" actually meant "The Meadows", but word about this place did not get out until John Fremont, who was an explorer, spread the word in 1844. Ironically, this same Fremont character had a huge impact in the Deaf world with the founding of the California School for the Deaf in Fremont, California which was a city named after him.

All of Reggie's friends had heard his spiel about Vegas' history and three major reasons why it became a center for organized crime back in the 1930's. First, gambling was legalized in 1931. Second, state divorce laws became very lax and "quickie divorces" only took weeks to obtain, whereas it used to take months or years before. Third, Hoover Dam was built. It was amazing how quickly Vegas grew as a city and it even obtained the moniker "Sin City" with the entertainment, gambling, and prostitution prevalent in later years.

His girlfriend, Pamela, had moved in about a year ago. They met online at some deaf singles website. He had almost never joined that website, but they had a "founder's special" because they were trying to entice people into subscribing. He had thought about it and finally did join for only a $40 one-time fee. Later, that website started charging $20 a month, but he was allowed to remain as a member for years at no cost until recently, so he was very fortunate with this.

Pamela Doff was a really feisty woman who was the same age as he was. She was not the most beautiful woman, but she was pretty in her own right. She always dressed in the latest styles and had too many shoes for him to count. She even insisted on getting a manicure every two weeks and if she ever cracked a nail, there would be hell to pay! This was the very definition of "high-maintenance" and he hated it. God forbid they should take a trip. She would insist on bringing ten bags compared to maybe two for him.

She was a deaf child of deaf parents and their heritage went all the way back to Gallaudet University's beginnings. Her great-great-great-grandfather had been a student who studied under Edward Miner Gallaudet. So, her family linkage to the Deaf world (we call it "EYEth"—if you think about it, the hearing world uses ears to understand thus the name EARth) was long and storied. He had a lot to live up to with so many Kappa Gammas and Phi Epsilon Zetas in her family tree.

What are those Greek-sounding organizations, you ask? Not many hearing "outsiders" (those who have no connection to the Deaf world) have ever heard of this fraternity and sorority. They are based only at Gallaudet with no chapters at any other university. They were run by only deaf students and alumni. So many leaders in the deaf world came from those two organizations. What happened during rush was kept a secret and nobody really knew what happens when pledges go through the initiation phase. Rumors abounded, of course, but it was like Opus Dei. What happened in those Greek organizations stayed in-house. As Pamela was a member of Phi Epsilon Zeta, he really needed to be a strong Deaf role model and ASL user.

Walking across campus back to his house, he eyed buildings as he passed them. Most of them were still sparkling new with the establishment of LVCC. A few of them now had Halloween props on the lawn with pumpkins, fake gravestones, and the usual. Seeing a few students on the way, he nodded at them, never smiling. He saved his respect and admiration for those who became interpreting students at colleges such as Northeastern, Gallaudet, Gardner-Webb, and Bloomsburg. Those who reached the fluency level in ASL earned a smile from him. He knew that students sometimes wondered why he never smiled in class and if they could not figure out the answer, then that was their problem.

He did not really relish the idea of entering his house with Pamela there. She was often controlling and always tried to criticize him in everything he did. One time, she had ordered him to put a shirt on as it was unbecoming (at least to her) that he walk around shirtless even though it was over 100 degrees outside and the AC was not working.

Why did he stay with a woman like that? He had been hoping for something better to come along, but he could not argue that it was nice having some female company at home who could cook really well. Pamela had studied to become a chef, but did not follow through with her original plans. The sex wasn't bad either and he had certain male needs that needed to be met. She was now a realtor and still could cook really great stuff. His stomach won the argument over his heart so he was sticking by her for now. It was basically a relationship of convenience.

Only steps from the street, he spotted her 2012 Honda CRV and groaned. She was home! With the terrible housing market since 2008, Pamela had not been able to sell many houses, but they were fortunate because Reggie had done well in the stock market in the past and money was not really an issue at all. This was going to be fun. A hot day, Pamela at home, thank God they had no kids to deal with. Now, that would be a deal-breaker.

His hand gripped the doorknob and he took a deep breath, knowing it would be the last peaceful seconds of his existence until tomorrow morning. Sometimes he wondered if his stomach was worth all this headache. In the foyer, he put his books on the counter and looked around the first floor. On his left was the living room with its standard dining table and six chairs. He didn't believe in having too much furniture. On his right was the family room which he spent a lot of time in. The 46" Sony TV was on and something was playing, probably last night's "Nightline" via DVR. It was one of Pamela's favorite shows, her way of keeping up with the news on a daily basis. He liked to watch it also whenever he could. Just like Pamela to go ahead with viewing it without waiting for him to get home. Nice.

Out of the corner of his right eye, he saw a hand wave. For most hearing people, they would never have seen that as quickly as he did. In his experience, they were just not used to having to use their eyes in this fashion. Consequently, it took a lot longer before a hearing person's attention was diverted. It was funny how deaf people always greeted each other with arms waving or lights flashing. Hearing people sometimes had it easy with shout-outs. He envied them that one!

Turning to the kitchen which was through the doorway from the family room, he could smell dinner. Yum! It was quiche, a favorite dish of his. She could always come up with a great meal that made him more relaxed as he arrived home from work.

"How was your day?" Pamela's eyes fixated on him as she stood by the counter. Her hands rested on her hips. Sheesh, not even coming to him to give him a kiss on the lips or cheek. Par for the course. He wished he had someone more affectionate and knew he had blown his golden opportunity with Angie when he was a graduate student at Gallaudet. Now that had been a really good catch.

Reggie allowed himself to think back to when he was student teaching at the Rochester School for the Deaf in upstate New York. For the first two months, he had been totally miserable living in the basement of the boys' dorm. He had been required to tutor ten hours a week to pay for the room and board. That winter had been one snowstorm after another so he was basically stuck there with his car buried under all that snow. He also did not know anyone in the Rochester area and Gallaudet was many hours away. He had not wanted to take the chance of driving back and forth in this inclement weather.

The student teaching experience had been a nightmare until five weeks passed and there was an all-campus workshop for faculty revolving around some topic he had long forgotten about. It so happened that Angie and her roommate Eve were both at this same workshop, sitting at the same table as he was. His attention had been focused on Angie from the first second he saw her. She was absolutely gorgeous! Everyone knew who she was. They got to talking during the morning break and something had clicked between them.

As it turned out, the next two weeks were among the most amazing of his life. He spent most nights at Angie and Eve's rental house. The chemistry was so obvious to them and everyone else. It felt like they had always been together. Reggie felt so stupid for blowing this opportunity with Angie. She had invited him to meet her parents and spend time with her siblings.

She had even surprised him by showing up at his Gallaudet graduation in a red dress which was his favorite. She had met his parents and they really liked her. What happened after that was he fell in love with Eve, her roommate. Actually, it was more lust than love. It was the stupidest thing he ever did. Of course, Angie dumped him after that. He hoped that in a parallel universe, he and Angie were married and had kids of their own.

Reggie sighed as his mind came back to the present with Pamela. "Today was so-so, nothing to call home about. The first class this morning was really weird again. They keep voicing in class for no reason. It has been a struggle ever since that first day. I remember that I had noticed students eyeballing me when I walked into class and again when I walked out of the classroom. They were standing in the hallway passing around five-dollar bills. I could not figure that out. I still can't after two months. Whatever. The semester ends soon enough. It is already half over!" Shrugging his shoulders, he pivoted on his right sole and headed back into the family room. Figuring she was just not interested in further conversation, he plopped on the couch facing the TV. Ah, it felt so good to be home.

Feeling the floor shake, he knew Pamela was walking over to where he was sitting. She had this habit of stomping the floor when she was upset. It would be soon that he reached the breaking point of kicking her out to the curb with her clothes all over the lawn. He just felt bad for Pamela because she had moved to Vegas all the way from Phoenix just to live with him after they connected online. She had no friends here and no family while his entire family was here. His mind wandered to how his parents felt about Pamela. He sighed and gave it some more thought.

Chapter 5

His dad had revealed to him that he did not like Pamela that much and he had even made sure his feelings were known to Reggie when they had a private moment over lunch at the Luxor the previous weekend. It was at their favorite restaurant where they always met. Right now, it was on Reggie's mind even as he watched Pamela venting at him and he needed to go over the conversation with his dad. His mind started to zone Pamela out and he allowed himself to wander back to what he talked about with Dad last weekend at the Luxor. It had been a surreal meeting between them. He would not soon forget it. Everything had felt *wrong* about it from the second he saw Dad.

Over the years, he and his dad had lunch at the Strip frequently. They loved to eat at T&T (Tacos & Tequila) which was a Mexican-themed restaurant at the Luxor Hotel. Reggie had his own personal favorite, Moe's Southwest Grill, so that was a perfect choice for him. The chicken burrito at T&T was so delicious with a flour tortilla, jalapeno aioli, crema fresca, Cotija cheese, tomatillo sauce, and pico de gallo. He could recite the ingredients because they had been there so many times that he was able to recall them verbatim. His dad loved the carnitas which had slow-roasted pork with some kind of sauce, pickled onions, guacamole, black beans, and rice. They always left feeling full!

Dad was also a big drinker and usually got the Choke on the Smoke, definitely not for the faint of heart. When they had been here last time, he remembered some key words from the menu description: "big, bold, bad-ass margarita", "tequila's wild, smoky cousin", and "might put a hair or two on your chest". Dad had really liked it and Reggie had a taste of it, almost gagging on the burning sensation that slivered down his throat when he swallowed. It was very strong. He stuck with Coke with lime and knew that this would do the trick for him, cooling him off with the Vegas heat.

For some reason, Reggie felt a little out of sorts as they met inside that fateful day. He had not been able to shake the feeling that he was being watched and even followed. Glancing around him, he took a few seconds to admire the beauty of the Luxor's interior.

Criss Angel's poster was right near the entrance of the restaurant. He had seen the show a few times, always amazed at the illusions and enjoying the audience's reactions every time. It never got old for him. Dad was a good friend of Criss Angel's and had gotten Criss his penthouse suite as a result of negotiations with the Luxor. How had anyone even imagined a hotel like this, shaped like a pyramid with hotel rooms and an Egyptian theme for the interior? When Reggie was a kid, he had been intimidated by the huge Sphinx overseeing the front entrance of the hotel. He loved the decor, especially the bar which stood in the middle of the second floor near the escalator.

There was some kind of starry warped wooden inner-ceiling hovering over the bar. Literally hundreds of bottles stood on the counter and shelves with so many different kinds of liquor that he literally lost count the last time he tried to figure out how many types of drinks there were. Behind the bar was a huge 72" flat-screen TV on the wall blasting music. There was usually some new singing sensation featured from the Vegas shows. He wouldn't have been surprised if the hotel restaurant had some kind of secret agreement with the casinos all over the Strip to seduce customers to go to these shows.

When he walked into T&T that day, his dad was standing at the bar. He was dressed in his usual gray business suit, white shirt, and red tie. He always had such immaculate taste in attire, which Reggie had really never possessed. He waved Reggie over. This had never happened before, so Reggie was very surprised. Usually, they just met near the hostess stand. Dad always enjoyed walking behind a gorgeous woman who swayed her hips as she led them to the table. Reggie, like his dad, would have normally enjoyed it also. But not this time. Dad seemed impatient and distracted as Reggie walked over. He gave Reggie a bear hug and Reggie could feel something unique about this hug, as he felt squeezed. This was really different. Dad never had hugged him before. His eyes were also not the same. This time, instead of being happy-go-lucky, he had a concerned look on his face. This was not a good sign.

"Hi, Reggie! Good to see you as always, son." His dad had this great habit of talking a bit slower than usual, as he was usually a fast talker on the job and with his friends/family. But whenever Reggie was around, Dad made sure he was included in every conversation that Reggie was present for. He knew he was really lucky with his dad in this respect. He had heard stories from deaf friends and colleagues about their frustrations with parents and siblings who talked a mile a minute, as if they were not even around. It made Reggie pity them and he appreciated Dad's thoughtfulness.

"Dad, what is going on?" Reggie put his right hand on Dad's left shoulder and squeezed lightly. He wanted to show his solidarity and communicate that he felt connected. They had a really close relationship and Reggie wanted that to always be the case, no matter what happened. "Did something happen with Mom?" Reggie feared a divorce more than anything except for a terminal illness or death in the family. He could not picture himself with divorced parents like most of his friends. Nor could he see himself at a funeral for one of them. That was totally beyond his comprehension and he did not want to think about it. He had this obsession with death and was really afraid of it.

"Mom is fine, son. Nothing is going on with our marriage. No worries there!" He winked and Reggie breathed a sigh of relief. That was a moment's respite. Now he could not imagine what was wrong for Dad to break tradition and meet him with a stiff drink. "Come, let's just sit here at the bar and talk." He sat back on his barstool, facing Reggie at a forty-five degree angle, his left elbow resting on the bar. "Do you want a drink, Reggie? It's on me!"

"Diet Coke with lime, no ice. Same as always!"

Dad paused, taking a breath. "Are you sure? You may need a stiff drink when I tell you what's been on my mind. Let's get you a menu so you can pick something out. I remember when you tried my drink last time." He started laughing and it was contagious as Reggie joined in with his laughter. He always loved laughing with Dad, sharing moments like these. Nothing made Reggie feel as good, not even his all-too-rare high moments with Pamela. Wait, could this be what this was all about? If it was not about him and Mom, it definitely had to be about Pamela.

Reggie tried to remember when his parents first met her. They had been going out for a few months at the time and Pamela had just moved out here to live with him. The four of them had gone to T&T for dinner and Pamela had expressed her distaste for the restaurant. That had been an affront to Dad who loved to eat there. Mom liked this place also, although it was not her favorite.

Definitely this was why Dad had met him today. It had to be the reason.

"OK, Dad—I will have the Pomegrante Acai. Yum!" Reggie had always wanted to try this drink which featured a margarita with berry flavor and tequila and fresh lime. The menu boasted that it had ten times the antioxidants of pomegrantes and thirty times the antioxidants of red wine. It was served on the rocks. Sounded delicious! "Now what is going on that we had to meet here?" He was even more curious what Dad would say. One thing Reggie liked about Dad was he talked to him man-to-man, even when he was little. Dad never had talked down to him as if Dad were smarter or wiser because of his age. Dad treated him really well.

Reggie looked at him as he had done every day in his life. Today, it was through a new perspective, as Dad had broken their routine of meeting near the hostess stand. This was so unlike him! Reggie's curiosity was getting the better of him and he fidgeted. Reggie's back was to half of the restaurant which made him uncomfortable. Deaf people liked to be able to see everything in their environment so he decided it was the better option to move them to the edge of the bar where he'd be able to see the entire restaurant floor. Luckily, T&T had a spot near the front end where it was possible to eye everyone coming and going. This is one of those "deaf mannerisms" that hearing people sometimes find puzzling, but it does make sense when you think about it.

This reminded Reggie of a classroom rule in his ASL classes. He chuckled inwardly. Every semester, whenever a student first got up to go to the bathroom, Reggie had to stop him or her so he could write on the whiteboard about the "bathroom inform rule" which meant that anyone who wanted to leave for a bathroom break had to raise his or her hand to inform Reggie first before leaving. He told the students it was because he needed to know where everyone was at all times as if they were at home and there was a fire. How would he know everyone was out of the house? At home, if someone left the room to go somewhere else, he could not hear the footsteps, water faucet, toilet flushing, or doors opening and closing. Once he explained that, the students understood better.

"Dad, can we move over there?" Reggie pointed to the front end of the bar. "Remember, I need to see everything that is going on. Appreciate it, thanks!" He could see Dad's eyes widen momentarily and then he seemed to remember from the many times when Reggie was growing up that he had asked the same thing.

"Sure, son. That's fine. Whatever makes you comfortable."

Reggie felt a lot better once they had their new seats and they were sitting cozily. The bartender was nonplussed for a second then shrugged. She was one of those hot-looking women with blonde hair and what Reggie called "ample assets" like someone would find at Hooters. He knew this was just a ploy for tips from men who got to ogle whenever they came in. This reminded Reggie of Jennifer Love Hewitt on "Ghost Whisperer" as she wore all those revealing outfits for no apparent reason. He had been hooked on that show until Pamela caught on and forbade him from watching it.

"Now, as I was saying . . ." Dad looked uncomfortable. Reggie knew better than to interrupt him in his train of thought. Once, as a kid, he had made that mistake and vowed never to do it again. Dad had tunnel vision and if anyone got in the way of his attempt to say what was on his mind, he would give that person a huge piece of his mind. "How are things with you and Pamela?"

Reggie was not too surprised, as he had a hunch this was why Dad had summoned him here. But it was still enough to faze him, as he was a grown-up man who made his own decisions. Dad never had said anything about a girlfriend before to this extent. He never patronized Reggie in anything he did. Reggie had been very lucky. Once he hit high school age, it was up to Reggie where he went to school, whether he used hearing aids, whether he could sign or not. His parents believed in empowering him and that had made all the difference in his upbringing. Reggie was a very self-confident and self-assured person because of this.

"Pamela? You don't approve of her?" Reggie knew the answer, but needed to see Dad tell him in so many words how he felt about the relationship. It might be the straw that broke the camel's back, pushing Reggie to break up with her once and for all.

Dad waved his right hand through his hair. It was not gray yet even though he was pushing 60. People often commented that he looked like Peter Graves from "Mission Impossible" or Leslie Nielsen in "Naked Gun" who had a full set of hair even in his seventies. He had won in the lottery sweepstakes when it came to keeping his hair and that was a good sign for Reggie as he would become older and hopefully keep a full mane of silver hair that women seemed to like a lot.

"You are right, I do not approve of her. She is very . . . umm . . ." He evidently was looking for the right word to express about Pamela. Reggie decided to make it easier for him.

"Controlling? Bitchy? Bipolar?" The last word Reggie had added just in jest.

"Exactly! She tells you what to do all the time! I do not like it. Your mother does not like it either. We worry about you and don't want to see you get hurt." Dad looked relieved to get this off his chest and he sagged a bit once he finished his sentence. It was evidently very hard for him to express this to his son even though they were extremely close and had shared many things through the years.

"Wow, Dad. I am glad you mentioned this to me. Mom never said a word all this time either. How come she is not with us?" Now that Reggie thought about it, Mom really should be here to support Dad in his stand against Pamela. Mom was never one to shy away from expressing how she felt, no matter what Reggie would say or how he would react to her comments. In many ways, that was like Deaf culture, as Reggie often mentioned in ASL class by explaining "deaf-blunt" which is the opposite of how hearing people voice their thoughts in a roundabout way.

For example, if someone you knew gained a lot of weight, a hearing person would be as tactful as possible and say something like, "You look very different than the last time I saw you," hoping that this person would recognize the issue you were referring to. A deaf person would just come out with it and exclaim, "You got fat! What happened? Are you pregnant?" Many hearing people found this personally offensive, but if they knew and understood this was how deaf people expressed themselves, it would not be taken so seriously.

Dad nodded. "Good question. She just felt it was time for a man-to-man talk. She didn't want you to feel like we were ganging up on you, son." It never ceased to amaze Reggie how well he signed what he wanted to say. People often thought Maxwell Kelleher was deaf when they were together. Sometimes he had even caught snippets of what others were saying about them, usually in a negative light, and he would glare at those people.

Then the fun part came when Dad said something like, "How dare you talk about us like that! For your friggin' info, I am a proud . . . yes, damn proud . . . hearing father of a deaf son who is sitting with me. He has a masters degree and a college teaching job. What do YOU have?" Reggie loved it every time and it made him feel even more of a man. He always appreciated it from

Dad and once in a while liked to remind him that it never went unnoticed.

"OK, Dad. I was almost at the point of breaking up with her anyway. She flirts with other men even if we are at the same party. It really is humiliating. Plus, I cannot even imagine having kids with her. She is so controlling and always thinks she is 100% right!" Reggie nodded and went on to tell Dad a few recent stories about how Pamela treated him as if he were her child, not her boyfriend who lived with her.

"Another thing, Dad . . . good thing the lease is in my name so I can ask her to leave anytime I want. But it would prove to be rough and you may have to call the police." An idea came to Reggie and he hoped Dad would agree to do what he asked. "How about if you came with me as a witness at the house when I ask Pamela to leave? That way, I have someone who can corroborate my testimony if anything bad happens!"

Dad looked at Reggie blankly for a second then he smiled broadly. "Absolutely! S-U-R-E! I just fingerspelled that just to make sure you understood." It was obvious Dad was thrilled that Reggie had decided to break up with Pamela. Wait, was he picking up his cell phone and calling Mom? Of course he would do that, especially in front of Reggie.

"Dad . . ." He started to protest out loud. Then, he waved his hand in front of Dad's face. So what if that was not appropriate in Deaf culture. Reggie or anyone was supposed to just wave discreetly or knock the table to get his attention. But not this time. More direct measures were required as Reggie didn't want all of this to mushroom into a big deal too quickly. Word had a tendency to get out there and Pamela would find out. Mom had a good heart, but she was a gossip and there was no way Pamela could find out before Reggie got home.

"Dad . . ." Finally, Maxwell Kelleher looked at Reggie and clicked the "hang up" button. "Whew, I am glad you did not go ahead with the call. Remember, Mom tends to tell everyone what is happening. Let's get Pamela out of the house first then we can tell Mom. How about that?" Reggie saw Dad's facial expression tighten up in concentration, BUT then it was obvious he realized Reggie was right. He nodded vigorously and smacked the table with his right hand.

"Of course, of course. You are absolutely right about Mom. I am glad you reminded me. Now, when do you think you can get Pamela out of your house? How does that work?" He looked worried and he had every right to be. Pamela was head-strong, to say the least. She was very difficult and obstinate when she did not get her way. Reggie had many stories to tell and Dad knew them all from when Reggie had told him on previous occasions. This was something that would need to be planned. Reggie would have to contact the landlord and inform him about his wishes to evict Pamela. He also needed to call his attorney just to be on the safe side.

Reggie continued to stare at Dad and could feel that there was another topic Dad wanted to discuss with him. Reggie gave it a few more minutes, his eyes targeting Dad's face like two lasers. Reggie hoped Dad would be more up-front with him, but after these minutes passed, it looked like he would have to be the one who broached the subject.

"Um, Dad . . ." Reggie cleared his throat and scratched his forehead. How was he going to even start this, anyway? Dad's eyes looked at Reggie expectantly. There was complete transparency between them, as far as Reggie knew. It was time for him to ask about Dad's Mafia past, with the nagging feeling of being followed and watched in recent days and weeks.

"I just wanted to . . . for lack of a better phrase, *ask* if there is anything I should be on guard about lately due to your checkered past? For my safety and for Mom's as well." There. Reggie had said it. The elephant in the room just got bigger at that moment. He was not going to shirk away from the truth this time. He had made sure he had a determined look on his face to show Dad this was not going away. Not today.

Dad did not look too happy. Reggie could see the wrinkles on Dad's forehead and the gray hair that was starting to streak. He looked old today and very tired. Was he going to open up to Reggie about something Reggie had suspected for a while?

"Son . . . I have a story to share with you. It may take a while to tell. I think you are ready for it. I am not exactly proud of some things I have done in the past with my business relationships especially with the Mob. After all, this is Vegas!" The edges of his mouth curled up into a smile and his eyes shone. Reggie wished he could have been a fly on the wall watching Dad start from scratch as a young man, scratching and clawing his way up the ranks to become such a successful businessman today. Dad would never retire. Reggie could not see him relaxing by the pool in West Palm Beach, Florida. Not anytime soon!

This was going to be a side of Dad that Reggie had not seen before. He braced himself for the truth. "Reggie, I am going to sign the whole time and voice-off. I don't want anyone overhearing this. Do you understand?" He was signing already and Reggie understood this was very sensitive information.

He sighed deeply and leaned over the table, his face just a few inches from Reggie's. He mouthed, "Do . . . not . . . share . . . with . . . anyone." He sat back slowly and his expression was one of stone. He signed, "Understand?" with raised eyebrows and mouthed "capisce?" at the same time. Reggie nodded wordlessly and his heart was jackhammering already. This was what he'd been waiting for all these years. The Discussion was about to begin! It looked like their talk about Pamela had just been the appetizer. How long would they be here? Quite a while, possibly.

"What do you remember about my father, Reggie?" Dad's dad? Dear old Grandpa? What had that got to do with the Mafia? Now Reggie's curiosity was piqued even more. This was totally unexpected.

"Gramps? He was old! Always treated me with smiles, hugs, so much love. I still miss him today. He had a pretty good life in West Palm Beach when he retired. We had a lot of fun visiting him. Always had some jokes ready for me!"

Dad smiled as Reggie talked. Then, Dad's face became serious. "Gramps was not the innocent, passive, upstanding citizen that you thought he was. He was born in Chicago, as you already know . . . his wife Rosie, your grandmother, owned a restaurant that was very popular in that city. We called it Rosie's Place—and there were certain individuals who held frequent meetings there. This group was called the Family although we have no indication that Grandma Rosie was involved in their business dealings at all.

"When I was growing up, I can remember sitting at one of the other tables with my eyes fixated on all of the people there meeting my father at one time or another. I had no interest in becoming involved in these ventures. They were very dangerous especially with the Depression in the 1930's. Eliot Ness and the Untouchables were after everyone and anyone who was remotely involved in the making and selling of bootleg alcohol with Prohibition. Do you understand? P-R-O-H-I-B-I-T-I-O-N, the ban on any liquor in the United States. It was a very stupid amendment that was passed by these strait-laced Victorian holier-than-thou politicians. But I am getting myself off course . . ."

He took his glasses off, placed them on the table, and took a sip of the glass of water that was on the table. He looked at Reggie sadly and sighed again. "Are you understanding all of this? It is important background for my story."

Reggie nodded again. This was way beyond any expectations he had of what Dad would tell him. It was obvious that Dad was just getting started. People were walking past them as if they were not there. It was a good thing he was fluent in ASL, as nobody could overhear them. Dad's back was to everyone in the restaurant so even with the remote possibility of an FBI agent or a mobster being fluent in ASL, nobody could watch him sign across the table from Reggie. His eyes roved around the dining area. Nobody struck Reggie as a possible G-Man or mob enforcer. He'd seen enough of them as a kid to be able to spot one a mile away.

"OK . . . where was I? My mother, God bless her heart, stayed out of their business dealings. Unfortunately, my father was another story. He had a huge betting problem with the horses. It didn't matter where the races were. He was at the local parlor betting on 'sure things' that never seemed to pan out. Finally, one day, his marker came due. It was in the thousands of dollars. He had a choice. Pay up or sleep with the fishes! So, he did what many people did back then: he quit his job to work for the Family. He had to pay off his debts.

"He started small, helping to transport liquor from place to place in Chicago. He proved to be so adept at this that he was promoted to lieutenant under Capone's henchmen who were battling the FBI. He acquired a reputation for being a tough guy and merciless on anyone who made mistakes. He would forgive you the first time, but if you made the same mistake again, God help you. He made sure people learned a hard lesson so no more mistakes would be made.

"Did you know that his drivers were always deaf?" Seeing the surprise on Reggie's face, he chuckled and nodded vigorously. "Doesn't it make sense? Deaf drivers had no inkling of what was being said in the limos they drove for my father and his partners. It was pure genius. That was one reason why nobody could ever rat out my father while many of his business colleagues went to jail. Nobody knew the drivers were deaf!"

Reggie sat there, totally stunned. Ironic that within two generations, there would be him, a profoundly deaf person who was signing with Grandma and Grandpa Kelleher's son! He raised his right hand, palm facing Dad. "A minute please? I need to absorb all of this for a second. Let me drink some more of that Pomegrante Acai! OK, Dad . . ."

He took that as his cue to continue the story. "Grandpa was not a big man, as you can remember. He was short, but wiry. Nobody could outwrestle or outman him in the Family. People would call him 'The Ant'. Some thought it was because of his small physique, but we knew better. His enemies referred to him as 'The Pissant' and my father did not like that nickname at all. He got stuck with 'Ant' as the abbreviated version of 'Pissant'.

"As the years went by, I grew up to embrace the same Family in which my father was an integral part. I had to earn my stripes just like anyone else did back then. I was given no special treatment, no silver spoon in my mouth. I was always in trouble in school so when I was expelled in high school, that was how I got involved with the Family full-time. I still do not have a degree today, although I do have honorary doctorates because of my charity work.

"When I was 19, I caught the attention of the top guys in the Family. They put me in charge of the loan-sharking business out here in Vegas. That's how we ended up here and we have done very well. My top guy here, who I will leave nameless, was not above slicing, shooting, incinerating, burying alive, anything to scare his victims into cooperating with him and paying off their debts.

"I met your mother out here, as you already know. She was a waitress at one of the restaurants on the Strip. That place is long gone and there is the mini-golf course right on top of it. Remember, I used to take you to the 'Welcome to Las Vegas' welcome sign when we drove the station wagon?"

Reggie's mind started to reflect back to those days and he could remember Dad taking pictures of him and Mom under that big neon sign. "Yes, Dad. Those memories are so vivid!" No wonder they had gone to that spot a few times during his childhood. Memories were so plentiful for Dad right across the street, having met Mom there. Reggie had not known that before. Tears swelled up in his eyes. "Why didn't you ever tell me that before, Dad? You would think this was important to know!"

He nodded. "You are absolutely right, son. I should have told you long ago, but now at least you know. Your mother was a sight to behold back then. Many guys flirted with her, but she only had eyes for me. I am a lucky man to have married her and we had you! Now, to the most important point in my story . . .

"When I was promoted to the second-in-command of the Family's business in Vegas, we had a business to open. You had already been born so Mom was home with you, her hands full. You were just one toddler, but it felt like ten to her because of your deafness. She was always going to deaf events, picking up ASL, meeting deaf people, researching her options for you in terms of deaf education programs out here, ASL classes, whatnot. She is an amazing woman. What would we have done without her, I have no idea.

"Your mother was, and still is, an absolute saint. My first business venture was opening a jewelry and gift shop at the Luxor Hotel. I used your mother's maiden name to hide this business as long as I could from the Feds. Did you know that according to Nevada gaming regulations, any casino could lose its license if there were any ties to organized crime? I had many loans thrown my way, thanks to Grandpa. But the FBI came calling soon after, in spite of my attempts to avoid detection. Many people moved to Vegas at that time in search for the American Dream with all of the hotels and casinos being built. It felt like a new place was opening its doors every week. Very exciting time back then.

"This business with our store did very well and we hired several employees to man the store along with some security personnel. Our profits grew year after year. It was all smooth sailing until one day when you were around 15 years of age. We caught someone on our staff skimming the books and giving money to one of our competitors. As you can imagine, that person was fired right on the spot. I made a mistake running the store. As I was inside the Luxor, the wages for our employees were identical to those who worked at the hotel. That wasn't much money so they relied on tips and our employees had to look elsewhere for the big bucks. This one employee, who we caught, was an accountant. He was bribed by another store to reduce our cash flow. Guess who owned that other store?"

Reggie had no idea who Dad was talking about and Reggie shook his head without a word. Dad took a sharp look at him and seemed to be disappointed in his lack of trying.

"It was one of the other organized crime families. This hit us hard and I ended up taking the blame for allowing this to happen. The head of the Family gave me two choices. One, accept a demotion and become an employee, risking a prison stay. Two, quit the business and if I ever uttered a word about what I had done and seen all these years, I would be wearing cement shoes. C-E-M-E-N-T S-H-O-E-S. Understand what that means?" His eyebrows shot up as he waited to see what Reggie would say.

"Dad, I've seen the G-O-D-F-A-T-H-E-R, all three of them! What do you take me for? I didn't just crawl out from under a rock yesterday." Dad's face softened up and Reggie felt relieved. Dad was still in there somewhere. This was a very intense story and Reggie was not sure if it was almost over or not. It better not be like 'Breaking Bad' with Dad another Walter White.

"Because of my connections, I was never imprisoned. But this employee spent 20-odd years in prison for what he was found guilty of: cooking the books. I don't think he ever forgave me for letting him take the fall for this. I am going to email you a picture of him. His name is Tony Rocchino. We call him 'Rocks' partly because his brain is full of rocks! Plus his last name . . ."

He chuckled quietly and shook his head. "The memories . . . I am just happy I got out of the business. I could focus on Mom, you, my real estate. But I am nervous that Rocks is out of prison and may be looking for vengeance against me. So, be on the lookout. As soon as I am out of this hotel, I will text you his photo and also one of THE car that he usually drives."

That was quite a story that Dad told. Reggie had been right, feeling that someone was really following him. The goosebumps were all over his arms, back, and neck. Hopefully, this was something that they did not have to worry about. But Reggie would rather be aware than blissfully ignorant. It might save their lives. So what if it caused a few sleepless nights? It was worth it.

Chapter 6

Tony "Rocks" Rocchino was pissed and he made sure everyone knew it. A lot of people had told him he resembled Sylvester Stallone from head to toe. He was not that good looking to most women. His face could tell stories with the chiseled shapes that outlined it along with the many tattoos all over his body. His eyes looked like they would penetrate your very soul. He had stayed in shape all those years even though he drank a lot of alcohol, sometimes two or three bottles a day.

Sitting inside his motel room, he had all this pent-up anger boiling inside him and he did not do what to do for the next few hours before exacting revenge on that no-good Max Kelleher who helped put him away for many years for what was a minor transgression while Kelleher himself got off scot-free.

Rocks had had a cushy job inside the Luxor doing what he liked most: being a bean counter. He had been able to flirt with all of those beautiful waitresses who, for some unfathomable reason, thought it was cool and becoming to throw themselves at him in exchange for a free dinner and drink. He had lost count of how many women he had bedded in the time he worked there. But he had not met anyone that he wanted to spend his life with.

Once he was thrown in prison, his life became a real living hell. He had compared his existence to that of "Papillon" which was one of his favorite books when he spent hours and hours alone in his own cell, during the time his cellmate was out wheeling and dealing. Prison had been a horrible existence. His cellmate was one of the meanest prisoners in the whole facility so he had been cursed with being a whipping boy every day for what seemed to be an eternity. It had stopped only because his cellmate transferred to a maximum security prison due to his violent track record in their prison. He thought about Max and what kind of revenge he would have on him one day when he came out of prison.

He was finally here in Las Vegas only a few miles away from where he would be able to destroy Max's life once and for all. It would be too easy to just kill Max and be done with it. He wanted that bastard to suffer for what he did as his boss at the Luxor Hotel. He smiled at the brainstorm he had about killing Max's son. He knew Reggie was deaf so it would be very easy to just steal a car at night and go the hit-and-run route. That would leave no fingerprints or residue. Once he was done, he could ditch the car and disappear forever. He would feel so much better. Then, Max would suffer losing his only child and that would be just retribution!

He got up off the bed and tried to pace around the hotel room to get his blood circulating. Going to the bathroom, he rinsed his face with cold water. Then, he stared into the broken mirror and could not believe how much he had aged during the time he had been in prison. He had heard and seen how much a president of the United States aged during one or two terms, but what he looked like now was so much older than his actual age. He had showered just recently and wore brand-new clothes for his getaway, as he knew he would not be able to stop anywhere once he had committed his avenging.

He continued to look at his own mug and he smiled, revealing some missing teeth from when he was knocked around in prison. He had gone to the infirmary more often than any other prisoner, as far as he knew. What Max was about to go through would be even worse, as it meant the rest of his life without his beloved son. Rocks was not married, and had no kids, so he really had no connections to anyone on this planet. He planned to escape to Mexico, to the city of Zihuatanejo where he could spend the rest of his life sitting on the beach, drinking beer bottles with any name on them.

It was soon time. He had studied Reggie Kelleher's habits over the past couple of weeks. He had even tailed him to the Luxor Hotel. Was Reggie having a secret rendezvous behind his girlfriend's back? He really didn't care either way. It was just something he found intriguing. He hated Max Kelleher so much that he wanted him to really suffer. If that meant killing Reggie, so be it. He said a silent prayer for Reggie and apologized to God for what he was about to do.

Sighing, he pulled up his Levi jeans and smoothed out his checkered shirt that he had bought at Kohl's near the motel. It was finally time do what he had to do. He made sure he had the room keys and his wallet. It would not do for him to be pulled over and thrown back in jail just because he did not have his license. He had gotten it renewed when he got out of jail. The car was a drab vehicle, but would do the job. It was a really solid American car, the trusty Ford Mustang. The 2011 edition of this car was a really good one, in his opinion. It had a lot of horsepower and fast acceleration. Perfect for the job he was going to do today.

He really looked forward to this. Even if it was the last thing he ever did on this earth, it would be so worth it. His eyes spotted the last bottle of Jack Daniels that he had not touched yet. He was still nervous about this and had almost backed out this morning, but he knew he would resent being such a coward not doing this for his own honor. He seized the bottle and drained the whole contents. The liquid burned his throat as he guzzled it all down. He had had a few bottles since last night. Consequences be damned! He felt like he'd needed his old friend Jack D. to calm his nerves and so far it was doing the trick.

Opening the room door, he took a last look around the room and silently thanked God for this opportunity. He closed the door and walked the several steps to his car parked right outside. Once comfortably settled into his driver's seat, he made sure there was nobody behind him. An accident or a ticket would not be very convenient right now. He did feel a little unsteady and saw that his hands were trembling as they gripped the steering wheel. Should he really go ahead with this today? He felt the absolute need to follow through. Otherwise, he might chicken out and never go through with this.

He knew where Reggie lived. He had driven by a few times, thanks to the website where he had gotten the address. Zabasearch was a gold mine for information about anyone and it had been easy enough to find Reggie's address. As he passed block after block, his mood became lighter as he neared his destination. Finally, he reached the corner right near Reggie's house. What made it kind of tricky was that it was right on the edge of LVCC and there might be security cars driving by at the wrong time. He did A quick surveillance and there seemed to be nobody watching this area right now.

He parked a few houses away and kept the ignition on just in case. The stick was in park and he was ready anytime Reggie was visible. He licked his lips in anticipation of exacting this revenge that he had been waiting for all those years, reliving all over the suffering those fists in prison had landed on him. Every time a fist hit him, he had whispered to himself "Max Kelleher" repeatedly to remind himself to keep living so he could get out one day and return the favor in some fashion

Chapter 7

Dad and Reggie finished their drinks and chatted for a while. Reggie wondered how Sara was doing right now. Lucky her, no drama in her life. She led a hum-drum existence. No dating, at least not that he knew of. Her routine was exactly that: routine. She got to work every day at the same time. What a robotic existence it seemed to be. He was really curious about her previous experiences as a strict Catholic, but had never gotten any further than the cursory "it is a long story" phrase that she threw at him every time. He secretly had a slight crush on her. Nobody knew about it. He had made sure of it. Even people who were close to Sara had no inkling of this. His crush ignored the fact that Sara made no effort to show her real beauty, but Reggie knew it was there waiting to blossom for the right man.

It had been a struggle not to trust anyone with this secret, but he had managed to keep it to himself, feeling secure that nothing would ever happen. Sara was unapproachable because of his fear of ruining their relationship as friends and colleagues. Knowing the rules of harassment on any college campus, he never wanted to push the envelope with her. She was a long-time professor at LVCC so Reggie held his cards close to his chest. He vowed that one day he would find out the whole story.

Pulling himself back to the present, he realized the enormity of what he would have to do in the next few days. Knowing that Pamela was working overtime tomorrow at her job, Reggie excused himself off the couch and told her he wanted to go talk to the neighbor about something. She shrugged her shoulders and walked back into the kitchen. He watched her walk casually like she had no care in the world. Was she really that unsuspecting?

Whew, it didn't look like she suspected anything. He hoped that Dad would follow through and be at his phone when he went over to Mr. Meadows' house to call Dad. He did not dare bring his iPad with him, but with the iPhone, he was able to use Facetime to call Dad and talk to him. Luckily, his parents both had iPhones and they had both bought one just to communicate with him.

His heart had never beat so fast as he stepped outside. It was cooler now in the late afternoon. Mr. Meadows lived down the block, approximately a five-minute walk from his house. He was a former military guy who had been a medical professional. He was now retired and stayed home all the time. Reggie knew that Mr. Meadows could be counted upon to be around for this emergency phone call that he would make to Dad and get the ball rolling on Pamela's eviction. It was very easy to saunter down the street with this brand-new sidewalk. Before, everyone would have to walk on the street itself and it was dangerous. There had been a couple of hit-and-runs in the past few years in the neighborhood.

Mr. Meadows was just a few more houses away. Reggie was very excited to get himself free of Pamela. He could remember last week when they had been at the movies. There was an open-captioned showing of "Avatar" and it was packed to the last seat. They had been there early, and Pamela had asked him if he wanted some popcorn and soda. He had nodded and said, "Large size for both!" He would never forget what she did next. It was totally humiliating. She turned to him and signed so everyone could see it. Basically what she said back to him was that he was getting too fat and she would only get a medium sized popcorn to share with him along with a medium soda. Over a hundred deaf people saw that and it ruined the whole evening for him.

Gleefully, Reggie rubbed his hands together. Now Mr. Meadows was just the next house over. What was that? He had the feeling that something was totally wrong. A rush of air suddenly whooshed through him. A looming shadow appeared on the sidewalk to his right and he turned around quickly. It was like this big monster almost right on top of him. That guy at the wheel looked really familiar. In the few milliseconds that their eyes met, Reggie suddenly knew this was Rocks, the guy Dad had warned him about. Shit! As usual, Dad had been right on target. Reggie's lightning reflexes kicked in and he quickly jumped as far away as he could, as Rocks was driving erratically and for some reason, the car was not directly aimed at him. The car Rocks was driving barreled down on Reggie and it was strange that he didn't feel any pain as the driver's side grazed him. Momentarily, Reggie wondered why Rocks had not hit him dead-on which would have automatically killed him. Right after that, he barely had time to scream and everything went black.

Chapter 8

Sara Zaslow sat at her desk, looking out the window. She had just seen Reggie leave awhile ago after checking his mailbox. Over the years of working together, she knew his every habit and tendency. He was sometimes predictable, sometimes not. All she knew was that students sometimes came into the office to complain about his condescending attitude towards them, as he never smiled. He did not make himself available to them. This last thing really surprised her because he was a deaf person and represented the deaf world to the students.

Also, she knew that Reggie had a good heart and cared about people close to him. He was very introspective and rarely went out for parties and holiday gatherings. He kept to himself a lot and had few friends. She was very fond of him and always enjoyed their time together. Unfortunately, he had a girlfriend so her feelings were moot. She had tried to figure this out many times over the years, but had given up when Reggie never revealed anything. But she was no better. He had asked her about the Catholic upbringing and why she was who she was today. Shrugging her shoulders, she reminisced on what had brought her to LVCC.

As the only child of two alcoholic parents, she had grown up in a totally dysfunctional family. Her father had thought nothing of throwing her mother around like a Raggedy Ann doll across the room and beating her within an inch of her life on a regular basis. Sara became accustomed to seeing black and blue marks all over her mother because of these beatings and humiliations. To her father, Mama was just "chattel", as in property. She was not allowed to go out anywhere without informing Pop. He had her on a real leash even though she could have broken free anytime.

She had never known Pop to show any morsel of kindness towards Mama or even herself in all these years of growing up in a small town that featured only one movie theater and one pharmacy. She could remember Mama's screams and moans at the mercy of Pop every night when he came home drunk from the local pub. He would drink there after work with his buddies, watching football or leering at the gorgeous waitresses who worked at this pub which was actually a sleazy dive at the other end of town.

Mama had no income, thus she was really unable to leave Pop and go out on her own. Her parents were already gone and she did not keep in touch with her siblings who lived far away. If by any chance Mama did get away, she knew she would have to eventually come back home to Pop's relentless fury. Pop hated his job as a custodian for some company. He went into different office buildings and felt that he was working beneath himself by cleaning ashtrays and sweeping, vacuuming, dusting, and whatnot. He was not a stupid man, but he had not pursued his education. He took it all out on poor Mama. He had made one stupid mistake, getting her pregnant at only fifteen years of age. At the time, it was expected that the father marry the mother so he had done that at only sixteen.

Sara could still vividly remember feeling terrified with the covers over her as she lay still on her bed, cowering in fear at the thought that Pop would come into the room and start beating her when she was old enough. Luckily, he had never done that. However, he verbally berated her and threw all kinds of insults at her. His favorites included: "You are nothing but a worthless piece of scum to me," "You will never amount to anything except an ugly, freckled, buck-toothed duckling," and even "What the hell was I thinking when I knocked up your mother and we had you? I wanted a son, damnit!" That last one had hurt the most of all.

She grew up a tomboy, playing sports that were mostly relegated to boys such as baseball. Softball, to Pop, was for sissies and pansies who did not want to crack their manicured fingernails. Every time Mama had asked for permission to go to the local manicurist, Pop had sneered and told her absolutely not. The only time Pop even treated Sara halfway decently was when he was there to watch her partake in school sports. She lettered in girls volleyball, boys baseball, girls soccer, field hockey, and lacrosse. When there was no girls' team, as her town was too small to have enough students for one, she went onto the boys' team even if she had to sit on the bench most of the time.

Staying on the bench was fine with her. That meant she was still on the team. It was a way to stay out of the house until after dinner. She would not have to watch her parents as master and servant. She hated to see Mama be treated like that and vowed to never allow a man to do the same to her. Her defensive walls were so high that it was impossible for anyone, especially a suitor, to climb over them. Many times, her teammates and coaches went out to the local restaurants where the coaches treated the team to dinner to applaud their effort. Sara was thus able to avoid eating at home, having to sit between Pop and Mama. The tension at home was so thick that one could cut through it with a knife.

As a result of her involvement with sports and more-than-decent grades, plus her dazzling performance on the

SAT's, she received a full volleyball scholarship to the University of Las Vegas which was one of the top teams in the country. This had saved her from a miserable life in the Wisconsin small hick town where she grew up. She did not miss the horrible winters when she would be freezing every day and had to bundle up in three or four layers of clothing just to stay warm. She was able to get out of that life in which her mother was perpetually stuck. The first day of college for Sara had been like a breath of fresh air. She could remember when she got off the airplane upon arriving in Nevada. She had just one suitcase with her, leaving everything else behind in her old life. When she stepped outside where the taxis were, the hot and dry air had hit her like she was in an oven.

She remembered how surprised she had been to see how much stuff her roommates and everyone else in the dorm brought with them on moving-in day. Everyone else had parents with them and that made her sad, but more determined to make something of herself. The first year had been a huge struggle, searching for her own identity as a person who was away from home for the first time. There was a lot of growing up to do and there was even a "cleansing" of her soul which was still an ongoing process. She saw a poster one day on a bulletin board for a support group for those who grew up in a dysfunctional and/or abusive home. She immediately signed up for it and that had been the best thing she did all year. She attended all meetings and learned a lot about statistics related to domestic abuse.

She felt very fortunate because she had survived a childhood without herself being pummeled or hurt. She knew many children were killed or permanently disfigured as a result of harm inflicted by a parent, more likely the father in the household. Abuse killed more children in America than accidental falls, drowning, suffocation on food, or fires in the home. She could recite statistics from memory after a year of being active in the support group. Over two million children were abused in a home over one year's time, four children died every day from domestic abuse injuries, and one out of four girls were molested by the age of eighteen. The statistics were downright frightening.

She was actually doing all men a favor by not having a boyfriend. She did want to break this cycle of abuse that she had grown up with, but she just could not stand having a boyfriend who was nice to her. She did not feel comfortable with anyone holding her hand and hugging her. Even a kiss out of the blue frightened her. She half-expected a man who was close to her to suddenly slap her face for no apparent reason just like Pop had done to Mama on many occasions. She simply felt too broken to be fixed by anyone. It would take a man many years to get her to the point where she felt at ease. She could not even be in the same room with men in general. She was always tiptoeing on eggshells because of her upbringing.

After college, she decided to take a break from men. She enrolled in an intensive Catholic program at a convent that was near UNLV. She had weighed the option of entering a religious order. But a few weeks into her program, she had been faced with a precarious, life-threatening situation that had almost killed her. She was assaulted by a seminary student when they were the only ones in the library basement. Nobody had been around to hear the screams and it was only after a vicious scuffle that she had escaped anything more serious than a few scratches and one black and blue eye that she was able to cover up with some blush on her face. It was then and there that she vowed to leave the seminary and return to the real world.

Sara was very good at maintaining appearances with a "poker face." Nobody knew her secret except for a couple of very close girlfriends at work who were in a different department. Reggie had no inkling about any of this and she planned to keep it this way. She had decided to tell her roommate after a couple of months of careful deliberation. It was important because they interacted on a daily basis and Jeannie had tried to set her up with guys who she knew on campus. She could remember the day she revealed to Jeannie the "battered woman syndrome" that had impacted her life in such a big way. She had even gone to a college counselor for this issue and thought she would improve, but she never had.

She could remember the first time she had ever encountered ASL and Deaf culture. It was in her sophomore year when she looked up classes to satisfy her humanities elective in college. There was an ASL I section open in the evening which was perfect, as she had to work. It met twice a week for 1 ½ hours so she figured she could swing that. It was right after Deaf President Now, the movement that had seen Gallaudet University get its first deaf president in I. King Jordan back in 1988. She picked up ASL very quickly, as she was a visual learner. She never looked back and decided to make ASL and Deaf Studies her future career.

There were many things that she learned in her studies. Would she ever consider dating a deaf man? She thought definitely not until she met Reggie. For some reason, she was really attracted to him, but he was living with someone named Pamela which was just as well. Would it have worked out between her and Reggie? She remembered in Deaf Culture when Professor Matheson had mentioned some differences between hearing and deaf culture. For one, deaf people were much more blunt than hearing people were. She chuckled thinking how students complained about Reggie's blunt comments to them both in and out of class. They just did not understand yet.

Also, deaf people often were late according to Deaf Standard Time (DST). It took deaf people forever to say goodbye to each other. Hearing people did not understand that it was very precious for deaf people to mingle among themselves and delay going back to the "real world" afterwards. Lastly, eye contact was very important in Deaf culture. She often saw hearing people converse without even looking at each other once. She did not like that. She very much preferred the "deaf way" of conversing.

Also, facial expressions made up seventy percent of American Sign Language (ASL), as it was crucial for signers to use a wide variety of facial expressions to accompany signs. Hearing people used voice intonation to add inflection to the points they were trying to get across. For example, a hearing person would use a sad or melancholy voice that was soft and tender when consoling someone at a funeral. A deaf person was unable to hear that so it would be important to express that by showing a sad face.

Was Reggie dating Pamela because she was a deaf child of deaf parents? In deaf culture, anyone who was a "deaf of deaf" usually was among the elite in Eyeth. Fair or unfair, that was the way it was. She had studied up on deaf history while learning ASL even though it was not on the tests she took when taking ASL classes. In her opinion, the tests had been too easy. She knew Pamela had a dominant deaf gene which meant it was very likely she would have at least one deaf child in the future, no matter what Reggie's genes were.

Sara knew of the unique challenges inherent in raising a deaf child, but that would never stop her from marrying someone who came from a deaf family that featured a strong deaf gene. She knew that the average deaf high school graduate finished high school with a fourth grade reading level. This had not changed very much throughout the 1800's and 1900's and it was true now even in 2011. The mode of communication used at schools for the deaf went from pure ASL, used between 1817 (when Laurent Clerc and Thomas H. Gallaudet founded the American School for the Deaf) and 1880 (the Milan Conference outlawed the use of ASL in schools for the deaf and just about all deaf teachers were fired thanks to the actions of Alexander G. Bell who was ironically one of the most admired icons in hearing culture) to oralism which stressed speech and auditory training.

Fortunately, the spectrum shifted back to ASL in the early 1980's after many years of study that resulted in ASL being recognized as a bona-fide language in its own respect. Ironically enough, it had been a hearing non-signer named William Stokoe who had spurred this shift. He was laughed at and scorned until people started to read his research. Without Stokoe, who knows when ASL would have been recognized, if ever?

What happened in 1880? Sara still could not believe it actually happened. She made it a huge portion of her Deaf Culture class every semester. She told students that it was like a Holocaust that happened to the Deaf world, a genocide in the making thanks to Alexander G. Bell. She was steamed about it because of the adverse effect on deaf education and culture which took over one hundred years to finally repair. The effects were being felt even today in 2011! There had been an international conference in Milan, Italy, in September of 1880. Alexander G. Bell supported the oralism philosophy. His fiercest opponent was Edward Miner Gallaudet who along with his father, Thomas Hopkins Gallaudet, supported sign language. During the conference, Bell succeeded in passing a resolution banning sign language. Only the United States and Britain opposed it.

This conference was the beginning of the dark ages of deaf education, as seen by sign language supporters. Resolutions avowed the superiority of oralism over sign language. This harked back to the ancient Greeks and Hebrews who had equated speech with intelligence. The entire conference had been a "fix" because the organizers were against sign language. The majority of the planning committee consisted of oralists from France and Italy.

What were the immediate effects of the Milan Conference? Other than all deaf teachers being fired from their jobs, sign language was banned in almost all schools for the deaf. The National Association of the Deaf (NAD) grew in membership, as deaf people who favored sign language fought against the growing oralism movement led by Bell. The major reason why sign language survived was the decision of Gallaudet College's president to preserve ASL on campus. Sara bristled at the thought of Bell. When she was growing up, she had idolized Bell as the inventor of the telephone. Ironically enough, he had been married to a deaf woman and believed that deaf people should not marry each other. He had thought that if deaf people did intermarry, the number of deaf people would grow due to genes.

Enough of Reggie. Time to teach her Deaf Culture class. For some reason, the college felt it was better for her to teach it, not Reggie. She suspected it was money. Interpreters are very expensive and she had fought against the administration on this issue because she felt it was much more appropriate for Reggie to teach it, as he was a profoundly deaf person while she was hearing. But they had not budged so she was stuck with it. She didn't mind, as she took a break from signing and voiced the entire class. Students always flocked to her section of Deaf Culture because they learned a lot about deafness, its culture and history.

She wondered how Reggie was faring after he finished his classes. Was he at home across the campus? How she longed to go over there and say hello, but there was Pamela to deal with. The days were always the same, teaching her classes and going home to watch her favorite TV shows on DVR. It was practically the only thing she did that counted for excitement, plus going to the library. She had no life. She should just get a dog and stay busy taking care of it with feeding, walking, and going to the vet. It would feel nice taking care of someone else. What would it be like to date Reggie? She probably would never find out, much to her regret. It took everything she had to maintain her composure every time he was around. He definitely had no idea how she felt about him.

Mercifully, the hours passed quickly and before she knew it, classes had ended at 5 p.m. for the day. Even though it was just the first day of the semester, it was still a surprise that nobody had walked into the office and mouthed off about how mean Reggie was. She sank into her leather armchair and sighed. The sun was still shining and it felt so hot coming through the windows. Time to go home for another night of TV boredom and Hormel dinner.

The phone rang, waking her from her reverie. A phone call at this late afternoon time? That was very unusual. Was it a deaf person or a hearing person? With Reggie and her sharing the same office, one never knew. It was pretty funny because if it were a VideoPhone call, she would need to turn on Reggie's TV and click on the Sorenson VideoPhone. It was a really cool device and many deaf people had one of these at home. LVCC had been very gracious to Reggie a couple of years ago, allowing Sorenson to install one in their office so he would have equal access.

Picking up the receiver, she could hear the frantic tone of the caller. It was the department secretary. What was going on? Did she hear this right? Reggie had been hit by a car or truck which sped off after the collision? Holy crap! He was being taken to Spring Valley Memorial which was only a few minutes away. It turned out that one of Reggie's emergency contacts in his wallet was Sara with both the office number at LVCC and her text number just in case the phone call did not get ahold of her. Sara's mind went blank and she could not believe that Reggie was in the ER right now or on his way in an ambulance. She could not think straight.

Just to imagine that she would never get to express her feelings to Reggie after all these years! That, to her, was unthinkable. Now, how to get to the hospital? She had been there before on an interpreting job and knew it was right near Tropicana and Flamingo, south of 95. She grabbed her purse and stormed out of her office. People in the hallway were surprised to see her running, but she didn't care at this point with Reggie so sick. Was he near death? She had no way of knowing, but wasn't taking any chances.

Chapter 9

Lindsay Veniglio finally got home after being at LVCC all day. She was still reeling from the first day of ASL class, but she had learned so much this semester. Reggie always liked to make her class laugh. Her favorite was when he told them that he was only twenty-one years old. The students, including her, shook their heads and some even signed NO. She smiled at the memory. He had written on the board "I AM 21 YEARS OLD WITH ___ LIFE EXPERIENCE"

So much information had been shared by Rego that she knew would be on the exams. She needed to absorb all of this information and go to the lab for the "Signs of Respect" DVD. She dreaded those hours in the lab and also did not relish the prospect of reading two books along with doing homework assignments in the Signing Naturally workbook. It was going to be a long semester for sure.

Now she had to look at the assignment for next class. Sighing, she knew each class was going to be tougher than she expected. She remembered when she skimmed through Rego's syllabus. Maximum of three absences all semester? Cannot be late more than ten minutes? Cannot be tardy on test days? Those had been tough to deal with, plus some people in the class even voiced when

Rego's back was toward them as he wrote on the whiteboard. She found it so distracting!

"Hi, Mom!" She sat at her desk, hearing footsteps just outside her opened bedroom door. It was funny that everyone in her family had his or her own distinctive pitter-patter of the feet. Rego had mentioned that in class, requiring them to raise their hand if they had to leave the room for a bathroom trip. It did make sense to her because he wanted to know where everyone was at all times. What she would do without her hearing, she had often wondered to herself.

"How were your classes, honey?" Mom's head popped in the doorway. She loved her daughter and was really proud that Lindy, as they called her, was taking an ASL class. To her, that was a very brave thing because the learning was all visual, with no auditory part. She could never have done that. Back in the 1980's, when she was in college, ASL classes were very rare especially at UNLV where she had attended as a liberal arts major.

"It really is a lot of work in ASL class. I even have a hardass professor named Reggie and everyone calls him Rego." She proceeded to explain to her mom about his reputation. Suddenly, she heard the name "Reggie Kelleher" and "hit and run" in the same sentence. Dropping her books, Lindsay ran out of her bedroom, almost shoving her mother to the floor. "I am so sorry! That was my teacher's name I just heard on the news. Hey . . ."

Lindsay sailed out the front door and ran to her car, getting in to drive. What hospital was it again? Yes, Spring Valley—it was not far from her and she wanted to be there even though she only had Reggie for two months of classes. Wait, was this the smart thing to do? Suddenly, someone was banging on her car window! She could only hear muffled voices. Sighing, she slid her window down and it was Mom.

"What are you doing?!? Get out of your car right this instant!" She knew Mom was very serious with her arms crossed on her chest. Anytime Mom's body posture was like that, she knew not to mess with her so she slowly got out of her car, but she was breathing hard and trying not to cry.

"My ASL teacher . . . news . . . car . . . hospital . . ." She could barely get the words out. This was the first time she knew anyone who was rushed to the ER. All of her grandparents and older relatives were alive. She had been lucky up to now not to experience this sinking feeling of knowing someone who might die. "I cannot believe it, Mom . . ." She so desperately needed arms around her and she stumbled around on the front lawn looking for Mom to hug her.

Chapter 10

Maxwell Kelleher sighed as he rubbed his forehead temples. It had been a long day since he arrived at his conference room at 7 this morning. There was a huge deal brewing with DeafWorld coming to town that winter. Someone was coming to sign a contract to book thousands of hotel rooms at a fixed rate for deaf and hearing people who would be flocking to Vegas in January for the first annual DeafWorld expo.

He remembered when he first heard about the negotiations and had missed out on the deal because he was at a family reunion. He vowed not to miss this second chance when the other realtor backed out due to financial reasons. The entrepreneur who was smart enough with a vision to set up something like this was an impressive young man who was deaf himself. His name was Bradford Hillson and he was coming in today with his associates to finalize all of the details.

Luckily, Max was fluent in ASL due to his son Reggie so there was no need for an interpreter at the conference today, nor had there been at any of the previous meetings. Bradford had been really impressed with a middle-aged hearing man who cared so much about the deaf community that he was an adept signer. That had won him over and this would drum up a lot of business commissions for Max. Silently thanking his son, Max got back to the forms and it was a very productive day with all of the meetings climaxing with the signed contracts which led to a round of champagne for him and Bradford.

He looked at the clock and it was already 5 p.m. Where had the time gone? He was expecting a call from Reggie any minute about evicting Pamela. He was excited that his son was listening to him for once. Sighing, he pushed his comfy leather office chair back as he closed his eyes for a few seconds. He was startled when the phone rang.

"Yes, this is Max Kelleher. Hi, Janice, what?" His secretary was not making much sense, but he could hear the panic in her voice. "What's going on? My son is in the ER at Spring Valley? What happened?" His senses were at full alert, emergency mode. What was this about Reggie? Hit by a car? "Oh Christ!!! I better get the hell out of here and speed over there. When did this happen? Just a short time ago?" Reggie must have been walking down the block to his favorite neighbor's house to call him, as they had agreed it was best to avoid the VideoPhone so Pamela would not know anything.

He had better call Vivian, his wife. She would definitely freak out. Wait, it would be better for him to drive home and pick her up because she would never be able to function on the roads knowing her son was in the ER. He knew where Spring Valley Hospital was. Luckily, it was right near the office and their home as well as LVCC. Reggie hated traffic and driving in general so that was why he lived so close to the college and everything else. It did make sense because he was unable to listen to the radio, so driving was really a boring chore for him. Were all deaf people the same way? He had wondered about that for a long time.

Their house on Decatur and Flamingo was a typical Vegas home with palm trees out front. There was only one floor, as he hated to climb steps like he had done while growing up. He came from a poor family and had worked his way up from the very bottom of society with old fashioned hard work, never turning down a job no matter how menial or backbreaking the work was.

He made it back home in record time and took a deep breath before going inside the house. "Viv? Are you here? I need to talk to you—it is important!" There she was in the living room on the couch. She was crying! Who had told her? Ah, the hospital had called her already and she was just sitting there, evidently too overcome to drive to there safely.

He stood right near her, looking down on the woman he loved more than anything in the world. The change in her was so dramatic. Just this morning, she had been carefree and happy-go-lucky when he left the house, having kissed her goodbye. It was amazing to see how life could change in one instant, like now. What was going on with Reggie at the hospital? Was he all right? A million questions rushed through his mind. He had just seen his son and their plan had been initiated, with him awaiting Reggie's call from the neighbor's house.

Ah, maybe he had been on his way to make the phone call when the car hit him out of nowhere. This was just not fair. Reggie was about to make the best decision of his life and now he was in the ER due to a hit and run. Who the heck had done such a horrendous thing? It better not be someone he knew or there would be hell to pay. Wait, it could have been Rocchino!

As that thought suddenly popped into his brain, he could feel knives sticking themselves all over him. He would never forgive himself for not taking the initiative to make sure his wife and son were safe from Rocks when he got out of prison. He would have to call the chief of police after arriving at the emergency room. Thankfully, he had many contacts in the Las Vegas police department, thanks to his previous involvement in the Family.

"Honey, let's go to the hospital right now!" Max slowly sat down on the sofa and put his right arm around his wife's shoulders. She was in a really bad state right now. Her eyes were puffy and red from crying. She sat there slumped over like the life had been sucked out of her. What were they going to do if something really bad happened to Reggie? He was their only child and one that they both had been so proud of, with his job as a professor at the local college teaching ASL.

It was not long before they showed up in the ER, anxiously looking around for a doctor or nurse who knew what was going on with Reggie. Max finally got ahold of the doctor who had treated Reggie when he came in. He seemed like a really nice and decent man. His name was Dr. Jeffrey Shapiro. Max sized him up. Shapiro was tall, gaunt, and was already bald even though he did not even look forty yet. Must've been all the stress from medical school and treating patients in the ER. That didn't surprise him. He could never have been able to handle that. They went into his office when things calmed down for a bit. The office was not far from the ICU where Reggie was sleeping in a bed, as a coma had been induced to treat his injuries which obviously were extensive.

Dr. Shapiro sat at his desk eyeing the couple coolly. He had been through many of these situations before in his ten years of ER medicine as a physician. He had been in the ER when Reggie Kelleher's body was brought in on a stretcher. It never became easier no matter how many times he did the notifying and explaining of each patient's situation.

Shapiro had graduated from the University of North Carolina at Chapel Hill fifteen years ago with a bachelors in chemistry and he went to Duke University Medical School. He had done his residency in neuroendocrinology, which was the study of the nervous system and how it interacted with the endocrine system. He also had done some work with advanced technical procedures which featured hard-to-treat brain conditions. In addition to his extensive training, he had authored or coauthored hundreds of papers for peer-reviewed medical journals and had presented at many medical conventions all around the country. All in all, he was the perfect doctor to treat the Kelleher son.

He knew who Reggie was by association to Maxwell Kelleher, the famous real estate mogul. This was going to be a sensitive case due to all of the publicity that was bound to result from Max's notoriety. Heck, even the Mob might get involved, as Max had been a member of that notorious brotherhood years back. He sincerely hoped that was not the case! He cleared his throat and braced himself for yet another tearful and emotional office discussion. It really was harder when the patient was a teen or young adult. It was not natural for parents to ponder the possibility of them outliving their child.

"Mr. and Mrs. Kelleher, I am sorry that your son is in this condition. We are doing all we can do to help him right now. He is in an induced coma for his own good at this time." He could hear sobbing and he resolved to continue on, no matter what. The sooner he explained things, the better. "He also has facial lacerations, a severe concussion, several cracked ribs, and a broken arm. Additionally, a lung was scraped and there is bruised heart muscle. He may have swelling in his brain and we need to watch that as well. There's something else I need to explain ...

"We need to perform a lumbar procedure and I need your consent to do this. We must extract a small amount of cerebrospinal fluid from the base of his spine. This is a clear, watery substance that runs along the surface of the spinal cord.

It also surrounds the brain, cushioning it from any impact. This is a huge concern with football players, boxers, and soccer players. I have seen this before. Car accidents are also very commonly associated with this procedure . . ."

What Dr. Shapiro was saying somehow was not getting through to Max and Vivian. They were overwhelmed by all of the information. Max finally understood that the doctor needed an OK for the lumbar procedure and he slowly nodded. Dr. Shapiro barked orders for the hospital personnel to wheel Reggie off immediately for the procedure.

Dr. Shapiro focused his attention back to the Kelleher parents. This was important to share with them. "The reason for this procedure is we need to check the clarity of the fluid to see if an infection or hemorrhage has take place. Do you understand?" He waited for the Kellehers to both nod at him.

"The car hit him going approximately 40 miles per hour. However, for some reason or other, the car just grazed him on impact and he is lucky to be alive right now."

Max could not believe what he was hearing. Was this the same person who was his son that the doctor was describing? He was beside himself, but he had to be strong for his wife who was doing much worse than he was. He felt as if he was having an out of body experience, feeling numb all over, as he continued listening to the doctor explain what was going on.

Dr. Shapiro took a quick look at the parents of this patient and he could see that the father was holding his own. Never mind the wife—at least one of them was still listening and not panicking. "It is very important that you two think one day at a time with your son in this condition. We are also going to take CT scans and x-rays later today once he has been stabilized and the lumbar procedure is done. Will he retain his memory? His motor functions? We have no idea right now. It is a guessing game . . .

"The brain is a complex machine and it is what gives us consciousness. It really is simple though, if you compare it to a TV. Once you pull the plug, the TV goes dead. I am sorry. Wish I could tell you more than this. Are there any questions?"

He hated to appear so collected and unemotional, but that was part of being a doctor. Perhaps it was not the best "bedside manner", but it would have to do for now. He felt like Mr. Spock in "Star Trek" who always appeared to be logical and detached. If he showed his emotions right now, he would have to feel the same way about every patient in the ER that he came across. That just was not possible for him to handle. The same went for any nurse or doctor that worked in either a hospital or office treating patients.

Max Kelleher felt more annoyed with each passing moment. This was just not acceptable. Were the doctors hiding something from him and his wife? He felt totally helpless which was a new experience for him. Even when Reggie was born, everything had been copacetic and he had been in the delivery room for everything. Doctors had later commented that they had never seen a birth that went so smoothly. Labor had only been a few hours when their son came into the world with very little pain and delay. It truly had been a miracle.

Was Reggie going to die? He was so young, not even forty yet. Max could just not bring himself to believe it. Minutes passed and they found themselves being led back to the ER waiting room. People came and went in a blur. Max just sat there immobile, not paying attention to the clock. His appointments could wait. He already had cleared his schedule for the day once he got the news. Nothing was more important than his son. He had so much invested in Reggie. The edges of his lips curled in a slight smile as he remembered decades ago when he had brought his son along to a casino for a mandatory meeting.

Oh, why hadn't he arranged for bodyguards for both his wife and son? Even if the possibility was remote, he really should have done that. Or he could have strongly encouraged Reggie to move back in with them and forget Pamela! The Family didn't care about her and he knew that they probably had bugged the house a while ago even though Reggie and his girlfriend were deaf, using ASL. They knew the couple watched a lot of TV so when it was on, that meant someone was home.

Burying his face in his hands, his mind reflected on the many years of raising Reggie. The ups and downs had been plentiful, but it was all worth it when Reggie graduated from high school, college, and graduate school at the top of his class. He had been a good son, always striving to do his best. He had steered Reggie away from working for the Family so there would be no trouble with the Mafioso. They were ruthless, those consiglieres. He could sense the dread spreading throughout his body, but he fought the feeling of panic and vowed to think positively for his son's survival and recovery.

Chapter 11

Reggie's body lay there in his bed unmoving, unblinking. Machines whirred around him to monitor his life signs. Nobody sat at the side of the bed as he seemingly was unaware of what was going on around him. However, nothing could be further from the truth. The moment he was hit, he actually felt like he was leaving his body and was being vacuumed upwards into the sky. He saw people running towards his body which was slumped on the front lawn of Meadows' house after the car took off. He had been able to see that it was Rocks and saw that it was a red Hyundai Elantra with Las Vegas plates. Ironically, there was a "World Peace 2011" bumper sticker on the back, right above the license plate.

Instantly, he found himself zooming upwards in a white tunnel. The walls were luminous and transparent even though Reggie knew they were also solid. The warmth was comforting and it felt like he was in a cocoon. He kept moving upwards and the walls felt further away from him. The light kept getting closer to him as he strained his head to look at it. It did not hurt his eyes even though it was the strongest light he had ever seen in his life. He remembered when, as a child, he had tried to stare into the sun. That really had blinded him and his parents had scolded him never to do that again, as people went blind from doing that. Not this time. The light was inviting, welcoming, all-encompassing.

Unlike anything he had ever experienced before. It felt like he was coming home.

He knew he was at the end of the tunnel as the walls disappeared and he felt like he was standing up. Looking down, there was no floor below him, but it was a hazy fog as if there were clouds. He had to laugh as it reminded him of "Heaven Can Wait" with Warren Beatty and James Mason in heaven. Strangely, he had no real body to speak of, but he had never felt more energetic or happy. He could see figures a distance away slowly coming towards him. Then, scenes out of his life flashed before him and for the human eye, it would have been impossible to comprehend these images. For some reason, he was able to do so in this condition.

Reggie could see far off that there were crystal buildings emanating rays of light. He instantly recalled the Crystal Cathedral in California where Reverend Robert Schuller had preached the Hour of Power. It reminded him a lot of that. There was no Jesus figure, no Saint Paul welcoming him to the heavenly gates. That surprised him a lot. Instantly, he thought of his grandparents! What about Arielle, his alleged sister that he had never met? Was she here to greet him as he passed over? Was she even real? Now that was a story. He had never told his parents or anyone about it.

Years ago, he went to a medium in Vegas who had a performance in MGM Grand. Friends had told him that Stella Frabizi could communicate with spirits that passed on. Stella had just come out with her own TV show called "Medium in Vegas" which instantly became one of the most popular cable shows on all of TV. She was a short woman and looked very Italian. She reminded him of his Grandma Rosie except for her blonde hair, but in a more modern way. She wore high heels and her shoes were glittery silver. Her dress was very tight. They were really eye-catching. Reggie had been surprised that her husband accepted her wearing a sexy dress like that.

She was not the most beautiful woman he'd ever seen, but she looked great at the show. Her hair was very wavy and silky. Her eyes looked like they would bore into your very soul. He hoped she would pick him out, but the odds were one in thousands, as the arena was totally packed that night. It had been quite an adventure to get into the arena. His interpreter friend Deanna had gone with him and the line snaked through the parking lot. It was a gorgeous day outside with nary a cloud in the sky.

Deanna believed strongly in this stuff, unlike him at the time. Reggie was one of those who really did not buy into this spirituality, the dead communicating with the living a la Haley Joel Osment who was amazing in "The Sixth Sense". But he had promised to keep an open mind. Deanna was a good influence on Reggie. When they first met at LVCC, she had been a fledgling ASL student who was married to a hearing husband who did not sign.

Luckily for her, the husband was very understanding and told her to pursue her dream of ASL fluency. Over the next several years, she was able to achieve certification as an ASL interpreter. She proceeded to teach her husband and two children some ASL. For Reggie, this was a notable achievement, as she had a full-time job, a family of her own, and many other commitments. Yet, she became fluent in ASL. He often used her example in his classes to show that anything was possible in terms of becoming fluent.

As they were sitting there in the audience, this medium immediately pointed in Reggie's direction. His eyes opened like saucers as the woman got off the stage and walked over to where Deanna and he were sitting. Deanna started fidgeting from side to side and even nudged Reggie in the ribs, with much excitement. Reggie kept Deanna in his peripheral vision so he could understand her signing, as his eyes were transfixed on the medium who kept him in her direct gaze. He was ready for anything or so he thought. Deanna tapped him hard on his right shoulder and signed, "She's talking to you, I think! She says she sees houses, buildings, deeds. Does your dad work in the Vegas real estate business?"

He gasped and nodded dumbly. He had never told Deanna anything about what his father did for a living. There was no way she could have relayed that information to the medium! His mind was a blank and he struggled to accept the reality that this medium was right next to them. There were even two cameramen filming the whole thing and a couple of others who he assumed were assistants with headphones and clipboards. They were furiously scribbling.

Deanna continued signing to him. "Yes! It is you she wants to talk to, Reggie! Were you thinking of eight spirits that you wanted to show up today?" He slowly turned to look at Deanna and did not know what to say.

"Are you kidding me right now? Yes! How did she know that?" He actually had been asking eight family members and friends to show up that morning as he got ready to go with Deanna. He had been thinking of Grandma Rosie, Grandpa Joe, Grandma Sam, and Grandpa Mal. Plus others who had passed on that were close to him. This was not just luck, guessing his father's profession and the eight spirits. Now what was next?

"OK . . . she is saying there are nine spirits here. Your paternal grandmother is standing here right next to you and her hands are resting on this girl's shoulders. I would guess she is seven or eight years old. Her name is Arielle. She actually named herself . . . she is quite funny and says she looks forward to meeting you when it is your time to cross over. Let me see if I get this right, she says she was miscarried and then your mother went away for a few months, trying to deal with the tragedy. Did you ever know that? You had not been in the house then, as you were away in school somewhere. College?" Deanna started crying and so did Reggie at the same time. It was a good thing that the stadium was dimly lit even though they basked in the bright lights of the cameras.

How in the world had this medium known about this? This was something that he had never learned about. It was true that Mom had been away for some time some years ago, but he had thought nothing of it. What he'd learned from Dad was that she had been very sick and needed some time away in an isolated hospital to avoid stress for a while.

Reggie had no idea that he may not have been an only child after all. After the medium's show, he had vowed to ask his parents about Arielle, but he had kept putting it off for months trying to figure out the right time to do it. Somehow, he never got around to it and now he was regretting his cowardice.

Standing on these clouds right now, Reggie looked around him and could see several figures become prominent in field of vision. Gasping, he saw Grandma Sam (short for Samantha) and Grandpa Mal (short for Malcolm), Mom's parents. They looked so young! He had only known them really as middle-aged and older. By the time he came along, they were both in very poor health. But now here they were, in their twenties from what he was able to see. Both of them were smiling broadly at him. Two more figures appeared next to them. Reggie could not believe it. Dad's parents, Grandma Rosie and Grandpa Joe! Who was that standing next to them? He had never seen her before in his life.

Grandma Rosie stood there, her right arm draped around a teenage girl's shoulders. This teenage girl ran up to Reggie and hugged him tightly. "Big Bro!" She was jumping up and down in excitement.

Reggie recoiled slightly and said, "What? Did I just hear that or . . . ?" He had never heard a sound before in his entire life, as he was born profoundly deaf. He had had no concept of what sound was. He was not really 'hearing' anything. It was like thoughts that passed through their minds. These thoughts had melodious tones that were so beautiful to listen to. But now, he had never heard anything so sweet a sound as this girl who was talking to him.

"I am your brother? Are you my sister that I never met?" Somehow, Reggie knew she was telling the truth. For some reason, he felt a holiness in this place where lying was impossible to do. The whole place was just beyond description. There were valleys, streams, forests, everything. The colors were amazing, even sharper than HDTV. His eyes could see every single thing so clearly. Were those people he also could see all around below him? They were so happy, singing, dancing, mingling, working.

He started crying. These were not tears of sadness. He was overwhelmed with such joy that he didn't know what to do with himself. Was he actually in heaven? All of his deceased relatives were here? This was the sister who he had never met! She was so beautiful! Even resembled him a little. Was all of this real? He vowed to try to remember everything he saw here, just to bear witness to it if he ever had to go back.

One thought did occur to him. There were no physical deformities in heaven. His grandparents looked like they were in their thirties. He remembered pictures of Grandpa Joe from Rosie's Place. Grandpa Joe had looked so strong and confident, like he did now. Wow, Grandma Rosie and Grandma Sam were so beautiful! Grandpa Malcolm looked radiant, looking at Reggie with evident pride.

Arielle was average height, but had very distinctive features. Mom when she was young had been blonder and taller and Arielle looked a lot like her. She would have been a head-turner if she had grown up. The medium had told Reggie about her previously when he watched with Deanna and he was so happy right then and there to actually meet Arielle. More relatives and some friends appeared. All of this was so perfect and Reggie was relieved that there was indeed something after everyone's existence on earth ended.

Was that a movie playing right in front of him? No, it was something else. He realized it was his life review! That was something he had heard about when watching others on TV who had a Near Death Experience (NDE) and he had never really taken much stock in that. His friend Deanna also had explained it to him in detail from her research. He had laughed it off then, even after his experience with the medium.

Arielle was just so beautiful as she stood next to Reggie. He could not keep his eyes off of her. She was dressed in a multi-colored outfit. It reminded HIM of Joseph's Technicolor robe, one that he'd seen at the Donny Osmond play on Broadway many years ago when he went to visit NYC with his parents. The play had been open-captioned due to the generosity of the Theatre Development Fund (TDF) and he'd never forgotten that experience. Arielle's face emanated such love for him. Reggie could see her looking at him with many emotions. It was not just love. It was much more than that. It was something higher and more advanced than anything he'd ever felt on earth.

But here he was, watching himself during his life review. On the screen, he was a seven year old during one of his infamous temper tantrums! He cringed as he remembered that incident being shown. He had been jealous of his best friend who was also deaf and hit him on the head with a plastic rifle. He could feel his friend's physical pain and emotional trauma. It hurt more than anything he had ever felt before. That scene dissipated and another one replaced it. This one had been a very close friend of his who he knew for a few years before they lost touch for a long time. He was now teaching at Gallaudet University in the business department.

Reggie stared at his ten-year-old self punching another boy in the playground and shoving dirt into his eyes. All this just because this other boy had chatted with a girl that he'd liked in their class. He knew right away who this other boy was. Now he owned a liquor store near the Strip and had a family of his own. The guilt had stayed with Reggie for a really long time. He had not realized how he was a hell-raiser sometimes! He could feel the sand and dirt settling into his eyes as if it were him in that boy's shoes. Oh, the pain! Humiliation as well!

Another scene popped up, one of him at seventeen years of age, at his graduation which had been a pool party. One of his deaf friends had teasingly pretended to try to push Reggie into a pool table and he actually had grabbed a cue stick to swing at him. Everyone, both hearing and deaf, had stared at Reggie as he snarled, "Don't you ever do that to me again!" Gosh, no wonder he had not been popular growing up. His temper was legendary and he had never realized the extent of it.

Was this going to be a life review that he found himself cringing at? He felt smaller and smaller as each scene manifested itself. What were Arielle and everyone else thinking of him? He slowly looked around and saw nothing but love on their faces. It was really amazing, the love and forgiveness that he felt from them, no matter what he had done. Even with the following scenes of games which he had played on Angie on a frequent basis, and including his infatuation with Eve. Ultimately, it had been up to her to go ahead with the breakup. Not him.

Then, a series of scenes from his LVCC classes passed before Reggie. He winced over and over as he felt the students' embarrassment, indignity, fear, hesitation, and many other negative emotions as they sat in his classroom. Gaping, he saw himself glaring at them and could even hear his own thoughts as they played out inside his mind. He could not believe how mean-spirited he seemed from the students' perspective. It was a miracle he still had his job and nobody had called him out on it. He could feel his face becoming red. Actually, he was quickly becoming mortified at what he was seeing, nevertheless.

Suddenly, he heard a voice from somewhere. Sight and sound blended together in such a way that it was impossible to distinguish between the two. This voice was full of authority. "Reggie, you need to go back now. We will see you when you come here again at the end of your earthly life. You got a glimpse of what happens in the next plane. Go, tell everyone what you saw. That is your mission now."

He suddenly felt panicky and did not want to leave, especially with his sister standing next to him in a bear hug. Oh, no! He wanted to stay here in such a beautiful, peaceful place. But then he could hear Arielle say, "It is OK, Reggie. We all will be here when you pass on. You will see me running towards you the very second you cross over! I love you and will be around you all the time."

His eyes swelled up and he could feel himself being swept up off his feet, going back through the tunnel. It was just like the experience he had had arriving in heaven, but in reverse. Feet first, he was zooming through the same tunnel which got smaller and smaller as he zipped along. Suddenly, he felt a jolt and really was in pain all over. Mentally, he screamed to go back to Arielle and his grandparents, plus everyone else he saw who had passed on.

Chapter 12

Reggie groaned and tried to open his eyes. It hurt to even breathe. He had never felt such pain in his whole life. Why had he been sent back? The voice that he heard had told him that his job was not done. He started to remember all of the not-so-nice things he had done in his life especially being mean to his students. He felt terrible and vowed not to let that happen again in his classroom. Wait, it was quiet again! Of course. He was able to hear in heaven and now he was back to being deaf again. This was just too funny. But his mind was clouded and he didn't think clearly at the time.

As his eyes slowly opened wider, he could see people sitting on both sides of the bed. His parents were there! How many days had passed? Weeks? What day was it? He felt better knowing there were others in the room to keep him company, but he could not remember names for some reason. His head turned slightly to his right and he saw Dad typing away on his iPad. Typical Dad! Always surfing for information related to his business, whatever it was. He just could not remember what it was.

Reggie replayed scenes in his life sequentially that he had seen up in heaven with everyone around him watching. So many times, he had been arrogant to others and even downright obnoxious! Strangely, in all of those memories, he did not communicate with anyone. What was up with that? He had felt like a spectator trapped outside as scenes in his life played for him, one by one. He saw so many mistakes and wrong choices that he just had to cringe.

What did he deserve to have such good parents being there for him? He cringed again as he remembered throwing out students only because they looked at their cell phones one or two times when they actually had just been checking the time. They had even told him they were looking at the time and did not have a watch. Nevertheless, he had stood his ground, asking them to leave. That was so ridiculous, looking back on that now.

His mind was on a roll. He had this really strict time restriction when it came to tests. If a student was even one minute late, he barred him or her from entering the room to take the test. This was true also for quizzes. For crying out loud! He had rationalized that the working world would treat students the same way. In fact, one of his students anonymously said on a professors' rating website that these students who complained about him were in for a rude awakening after graduation.

Oh, the students must hate him at LVCC! Not only did students despise him, he realized he could only imagine how other faculty and staff felt about him. The same was true for many people at work in his past jobs when he was around deaf and hearing people all day. He had had more than his share of conflicts and tensions in all of his jobs. Suddenly, he remembered his life review vaguely when he had been out of his body. With much effort, Reggie's right hand formed an "ILY" sign and he struggled to hoist his hand in the air. Unable to do so, he wiggled as much as he could to grab Dad's attention.

Reggie absolutely had to ask Dad about Arielle before Mom woke up from her nap. He could have whispered to Dad and asked him about whether the miscarriage was true or not, but in his heart and mind he knew it had happened. This was the only thing he could think about right now. His mind was racing and he could feel his heartbeat going a mile a minute. The thought that he had a sister up in heaven was squeezing his brain so hard that he could have sworn he had a real migraine for the first time, ever.

Chapter 13

Max Kelleher's eyes still couldn't stay dry for a few seconds at a time. It had been days since his son went into a coma. Would he ever wake up? Would he ever be able to embrace Reggie again? He looked like he had not showered for days and he really hadn't. Nobody ever before had ever seen Max in this disheveled state. Ever! He had prided himself on appearance, looking his very best with clothes and everything. There was never a strand of hair out of place.

Right now, it was the total opposite. His mind had a thousand questions all jumbled together. He had never felt so helpless even as he tried to work on his tablet for business purposes. The corner of his left eye caught some movement. What was that? Holy crap! Was it really happening? He saw the "ILY" hand shape and his brain refused to process it for a minute.

He became hyper and pushed his chair back. Yes! Reggie was doing their "secret sign". He flashed back to years ago when he dropped off his son at school. Their routine was that Reggie would close the car door and right before he walked into the school building, he would turn around to wave "ILY" to him. They did that through the years even when Reggie was in high school.

He was sure classmates had taunted Reggie for doing that, but it had never stopped him. Reggie always explained to people that it was a "deaf thing" that his parents understood, unlike the vast majority of hearing parents who had deaf children but never learned ASL. It became something of a badge of pride for Max, even when Reggie was an adult. He ran out of the room, yelling for a doctor.

Vivian Kelleher, his wife, who had been sleeping in her chair, sat up in bewilderment at this atypical behavior. Her husband was always so unflappable and cool in his demeanor. What was going on? In all her years of being married to Maxwell Kelleher, she had never seen him so distraught. But, then again, she had never felt this way before, either. Their son was in the hospital, all hooked up to different machines to keep him alive. He did not even look alive, with his skin so pasty white and all those tubes sticking out of him plus a breathing apparatus that was there to make sure he was getting enough oxygen.

Vivian was not what you would call beautiful even though she had been pretty when she was young. She had smoked for many years and it took a toll on her body and face. She kept putting on more and more makeup until it made no difference. Then, she gave up on that, yet Dad still loved her completely. She had an inferiority complex with her husband being around gorgeous women all the time in Vegas, but she had learned to trust him.

In fact, he never cheated on her throughout their marriage and thus her fears were put to rest gradually. She thought of Trump when comparing Max's appearance with the Donald's. They were a rock-solid couple who had stayed together even as their friends broke up one by one. Eventually, they were the only once-married couple remaining in their circle of friends. It really amazed her and she never thought this would have happened.

But, wait . . . was that Reggie's right hand in the "ILY" sign? Yes, it was! Never had she hoped for such a miracle. Her eyes were like saucers as she slowly moved them over to her son's face. His eyes were open and looking at her! Her heart fluttered and she was so happy. He was going to be okay! He was alive and that was all that mattered.

Suddenly, Reggie was thrashing on the bed! Vivian did not know what to do except yell for the doctors to come back. Dr. Shapiro was the first one to enter the room. When he saw what Reggie was doing, he knew right away what was going on.

"He doesn't need the breathing tube any more, Mr. and Mrs. Kelleher. I am going to remove it. His brain, along with the rest of his body, has just clicked on back to life."

Vivian watched with wonder along with Max as the doctor reached over, cut the securing tape, and carefully took out the breathing tube. She gasped as Reggie choked a little bit and took the first fully unaided lungful of air that he'd had in a few days. His eyes darted from right to left, finally resting on his parents.

But Reggie's head and face were very swollen and bruised. He had a cast on his left arm, which was broken. He was pretty much unrecognizable to anyone who did not know him very well. She would know Reggie anywhere even with the lips and ears black and blue. Yet, it was still Reggie laying there, as he had remembered the "ILY" secret code between him and Max. How much brain function was still there? Even the doctors did not know yet so she was hopeful now that they had gotten lucky this time.

Max stood in the room next to his wife, out of breath. He saw her smiling through her tears. "Is he still awake and with us?" He desperately wanted and hoped for his son to make it through this like nothing else ever mattered in his life. He would trade all of his real estate success and all of his investments for his son to be OK. This was all too good to be true. Had Dr. Shapiro actually extracted the breathing tube, signaling that Reggie was going to be OK?

"Yes, honey. Reggie is looking at me and blinking. It truly is a miracle!" Vivian was beside herself with joy. One thing at a time. If Reggie needed therapy, so be it. They would tackle it head on like they did anything else they came across when their son was growing up. They both were fluent in ASL and this was something that almost no other parents they met had ever achieved.

She got off her chair and massaged Reggie's left hand like she always had when he was upset or crying as a young child. She was hoping he would recognize this so he would know it was Mom sitting with him. "We're gonna get through this, R-E-G-G-I-E!" She signed as she talked to him. Tears came down her cheeks as she looked at her son laying in bed in front of her. "We're gonna stick together, son!" The hand squeezed hers back. Reggie was still in there somewhere! Vivian was overjoyed. It was yet another spark of life that she had seen in just a few minutes. Their son was a strong person.

Max watched this with wonder. Reggie really was unique, even if he was their son! Doctors, be damned. He was going to be fine. From his experience, doctors always were overcautious about a prognosis probably to save themselves from medical malpractice lawsuits. He had friends who practiced medicine and they all told him the same thing. Malpractice insurance premiums were beyond ridiculous these days so most doctors now were working for HMO's to avoid paying those high premiums.

The doctors explained to Max and Vivian that Reggie was not yet out of the woods. The most dangerous issue was the swelling in his brain, which restricted the blood flow to his brain cells. This meant that these cells were craving nutrients and oxygen that the brain normally provided.

Another concern was the dangerously low blood pressure which reduced the blood flow to vital organs including the brain.

There could be a drastic reduction of motor function, memory loss, and other complications. This was a sobering few minutes of explanation. At the end, Max and Vivian felt drained. From what they understood, the first forty-eight hours were the most critical. Once Reggie survived past that, the chances of complications would be much lower.

Max was a quick study and he had learned how to read all of the monitors in the room. He taught Vivian as he went along. All day, every day, they carefully watched the numbers and within a few more days, all was looking good for Reggie's recovery. There was nothing they could do to make him better. The hospital was very good to them, providing two cots in the room so they could stay with their son.

Max had a sudden thought. Was there a chapel in the hospital? He nudged Vivian and said, "I am going to see if there is a prayer chapel in this place. Would that be OK? We could even take turns going in there to pray to God for our son!" Vivian's eyes lit up and she nodded speechlessly. They were united in their resolve to see Reggie recover completely. Whatever it took! As part of their routine, they decided to frequent the chapel at least once a day to talk to God about Reggie's recovery.

Max found the chapel after asking for directions at the nurses' station. It was a maze and he chuckled just thinking how to describe it to Viv. She would need a GPS to find it. First things first. Entering the chapel, he liked it immediately. It was a simple looking room with wooden pews and a small podium for the speaker. Stained glass windows adorned the walls.

From his childhood, he recognized the different religious symbols—the cross, Star of David, and crescent—representing Christianity, Judaism, and Islam. There was an assortment of other religious symbols that he did not recognize, but they were probably from the eastern religions about which he had no clue.

He prayed for about fifteen minutes. His prayer went something like this, "God, please place your healing hands on our son Reggie. I have never prayed to you before, so I am making this up as I go along. I know I have not been attentive to you at all, but I am on my knees now begging you to listen. I know the saying that there is a Christian in every trench or something like that. Please give me a sign that everything will be all right. Thank you, Lord."

Going back to the room, he glanced at Viv who was sitting down in Reggie's room. Her elbows were on Reggie's bed and he immediately recognized the prayer stance without having to see more of this scene. Interesting that one didn't have to go to the chapel to talk to God. His eyes automatically went to the blood pressure monitor. Was he seeing things? The numbers were going down near normal range. Viv finished praying as he entered the room. She looked at the numbers too and smiled, turning to Max.

"He's going to be OK! That was a really important thing, his blood pressure. Now let's see about his brain swelling. He has a camino bolt drilled into his head to measure the pressure between his brain and skull. He is on morphine to dull the pain and the numbers on that are going down as well. It is a miracle!" Viv could not believe how much better Reggie was doing in such a short time. Max looked at her and nodded, smiling.

A nurse came into the room and announced they had two visitors. Max and Viv looked at each other and decided to go to the waiting room to see who these people were. They walked down the hallway and saw two women standing around, looking very uncomfortable. Who were these women? Reggie and Vivian recognized neither lady who was there, but it was obvious both of them cared enough about Reggie to come to the ER and ask about his welfare.

Max led Viv over to the women and introduced themselves. "Hello. We are Reggie's parents, Maxwell and Vivian Kelleher. Thank you both for coming. How do you know our son?"

Lindsay Veniglio cleared her throat and she felt very small standing next to Sara Zaslow, the ASL lab coordinator at LVCC, but she went ahead and talked first. "Hi, my name is Lindsay. I've had Mr. Kelleher as my ASL professor for this semester and I am also president of the ASL Club so I wanted to be here." She looked at Sara and nodded. She felt a little better having introduced herself briefly. "Oh, by the way, he is a very demanding professor and I've enjoyed his class!"

She had gone to his office many times during the semester, for extra help and she had really needed it. Her ASL skills had blossomed over the past couple of months, thanks to the frequent one-on-one conversations in which she struggled to utilize all of the signs and phrases she learned from Reggie's class.

Sara Zaslow smiled as she listened to Lindsay gush about Reggie. She was surprised, as she had checked different professor rating websites online which were a very entertaining resource on how good or bad a professor was. She did notice that she got a lot of remarks on how drab she was but at the same time teaching quite effectively while Reggie got what amounted to quite a bit of negative comments from students. Reggie also was infamous for wasting time on tangents that had nothing to do with the course itself.

"Thank you, Lindsay. That was very kind of you to come." Sara's eyes shifted from the young and petite student next to her and focused on Reggie's parents who looked so disheveled right now. She could not blame them. Their son was in serious critical condition. "My name is Sara Zaslow. I am Reggie's colleague and lab coordinator at LVCC. We share an office and have been working together for many years. How is he? What happened?" She asked the question with a sense of dread, hoping for the best and steeling herself for the worst.

Max looked at both women and was really impressed at the fact that Reggie had affected their lives in such a way that they were worried about him. "I think he is going to be OK. He was walking to another house on his block when a car hit him and took off. He was very lucky. The doctors are being overcautious, and I don't blame them, as it will be a long process until Reggie gets better. As he is in and out of a coma, they won't allow you both to see him, but I will definitely tell him you two came. Thank you so much!"

Sara was nonplussed. She wanted to see Reggie, but realized he was probably in very bad shape at this time. There was nothing much for her to do but to hope for him to recover fully. Who was going to teach his classes? That meant calling all of the adjunct professors to take up the slack. Money would not be an issue as LVCC had emergency funds in case of something like this. She had no doubt there would be a lawsuit so the money would not be missing forever.

Reggie was in a coma? That was not good, but at least he was alive. From what she sensed while his father spoke, she got the impression there was much to hope for. Feeling a renewed sense of purpose, she hugged Lindsay goodbye and went home to start calling the adjuncts to take over Reggie's classes. She missed him already and wished she had told him how she felt. She vowed to do it at the first opportunity once he was up and about on his feet. There was no more delaying the inevitable. She had never gotten married and she found herself in love with this deaf professor even with all of his faults. She knew he could be arrogant and opinionated, but she always felt comfortable with him and loved his sense of humor.

A few hours later, she was relieved. After making many phone calls, she got coverage for all of his classes except for the early morning one. That one she would take over. A bonus was that Lindsay was in it. She had been impressed with Lindsay's progress from day one and she was pretty confident that Lindsay would be fluent quickly because of her involvement with the ASL Club and her frequent attendance at deaf events. While the ASL classes only required two or three deaf events, Lindsay must have gone to several already in just two months.

Sighing, she sat back in her desk chair and stared at the iMac 21" with its beautiful screensavers. One by one, they showed pictures of different beaches. Her favorite was the rickety hut with two straw chairs facing the water.

She could easily imagine Reggie and herself enjoying a vacation or even a honeymoon together like that. But she was faced with another problem right now. There was another man, Marcus Brossler, in her life who was just a friend right now. They had dated for a while. He was an owner of a deli business and had worked his way up from being a delivery man. He really wanted to take things to the next level again, but she was not interested. He was a very successful businessman, but in her opinion, he drank too much and on a daily basis. She also had seen his volatile temper, yelling at the TV late at night during sports games. She did not feel comfortable sitting next to him when he did that.

He also spent a lot of time at male friends' houses and bars watching football games during the pro season. He even bet a lot of money at OTB on horse races. He would flirt shamelessly with waitresses and female customers he had never met before, even in front of her. This was not the type of man she wanted to have a relationship with. It was time to end it and for good.

She shook her head and laughed at something Marcus had told her one day as they argued about his drinking. He said he was a "functioning alcoholic", which meant he was just fine and went to work every day like nothing was happening. There had even been times when she tried to see him, but he preferred to go to a friend's for football games, drinking, pizza, and telling dirty jokes all day. That had really turned her off. It was time to end it right then and there.

She picked up her iPhone and dialed his number. She could hear the other end ringing a few times. He was not there! Relieved, she left a message saying she could not see him anymore because she was in love with someone else in her life. Hanging up with a decisive click, she felt better immediately. It was time to start focusing on Reggie's recovery and the ASL classes including Lindsay's. She smiled for the first time that whole day at the prospect of showing Reggie how much she felt for him as a friend and possibly more. But he had to get better first and that was going to be a long haul.

She could remember the abuse that Marcus had heaped upon her as well. She still couldn't believe she had tolerated it even once. Rationalizing it away became second nature to her. Every time she had a bruise and anyone asked her about it, she would say she fell or hit a door. Anything to keep the police away. She knew he was a very angry and physical man so she did not want to give him any provocation to take it out on her, but this was the end. She wanted Reggie, a man who was always so good to her in spite of his many faults. She would work with him on those.

She remembered one day at work really vividly. Having a bad morning, she arrived at their office desperately needing a laugh or relaxing moment with Reggie, away from everyone. However, he had been down that day as well, saying something negative as she walked in the door. She could not expect him to be happy all the time either. But she had sniped at him, "Hey, I needed something positive from you today, Reggie. That's the first time I've seen you negative!" The look on his face had been priceless. She wished she could take that back right now.

Chapter 14

Reggie knew that hours and days had passed from the window which showed day and night. Time began to feel like a blur. Where had he been after the accident? Struggling to remember, he slowly became more alert of his surroundings and was able to sit up in bed. His head was bandaged and he could not make any sense of what people were saying to him for some reason.

His brain was still cloudy at this point, but he vaguely remembered the bizarre experience he had had seeing Arielle and his grandparents. Had he seen and heard more? Was it a real occurrence or just a dream? Was it one of those instances where the brain, deprived of oxygen, was signaling that his life was coming to an end? He'd heard the debate before, but had never paid much attention to it.

Finally, the time came when he was able to start finding out what happened to him. Seeing Dad come in one morning, Reggie waved his right arm for Dad's attention. He had gotten some of his strength back. He tried to express himself in ASL, but for whatever reason, his hands and arms were not cooperating. Damn! What was going on here? He was an ASL professor, yet could not even formulate a single sign except for "ILY". How pathetic was that?

Luckily, he could speak and lipread pretty well so he had that to fall back on. "Dad, listen . . ." Reggie was still obsessed about asking Dad about having a sister. His eyes roamed around the room and he saw a newspaper spread out on a table near the chairs. He grimaced as it took effort for him to point to it and he pantomimed using a pen. Dad looked at him questioningly and after a few seconds, he understood. Reggie's hand held the pen unsteadily as he wrote "I HAVE SISTER MISCARRIED?" He could not really think straight at the time and dropped the pen on the table near his bed, already tired from exertion.

What he did not expect was Dad's face to whiten and his eyes to moisten. He nodded and started signing quickly. He looked around and Reggie guessed he was looking for Mom to see if she was around, but she wasn't.

"Reggie! How did you know about that? Why are you bringing it up now?"

What was Dad doing? His arms and hands moving around so quickly. Reggie had no idea what he was saying! Did he forget everything he'd learned his whole life with ASL? "Dad . . . this is very important . . ."

Dad's face crinkled in surprise at hearing Reggie's voice, hoarse as it was from the tube that had been taken out a couple of days ago. Dad definitely had not expected Reggie to be talking instead of signing. "For whatever reason, I cannot sign right now and I am scared because I don't remember any ASL!"

Dad stood near Reggie and shook his head. "I don't know, Reggie. Let me get the doctor for you and we'll talk about it. As for you having a sister, that is something we will have to talk about another time, especially with Mom not around. OK? But, yes, to be honest, she did miscarry . . . I would say fifteen years ago. You were already out of the house and Mom was too old to have another child . . ." His face looked pained and his body shook, especially his hands like Reggie had never seen before. He looked unsteady and lost.

Dad continued, "I will have to write everything down on paper. Do you understand signs?" Then, he moved his arms and hands to say something, but Reggie did not comprehend a single thing Dad was trying to say. What was going on here? Now he was in trouble! An idea popped into Reggie's head.

"Dad, can you type on your tablet while the doctor explains what is going on? Maybe that will help me follow along." Dad nodded vigorously and wagged his index finger at Reggie, winking in spite of the traumatic question that Reggie had asked about having a sister. The doctor came in and Reggie was surprised that Dad was able to summarize what Dr. Shapiro explained about his induced coma.

It turned out there were many different levels of coma and even now Reggie was classified as being in a coma, although he was alert for longer periods of time and talked a little bit. His throat was still going to be hoarse for a while. Then, he saw the doctor frown at something Dad asked him. Definitely was a question about why he couldn't comprehend nor express in signs.

Dad looked at Reggie and put up his palm as if he was to wait. Reggie knew what that meant. Dad would explain more in detail later. Reggie felt lucky because he had many deaf friends whose parents and siblings said, "Not important, tell you later" then never did. In Drolsbaugh's book and also Kane's, these authors did explain that and gave some situations as examples. As for Reggie, his parents consistently explained in depth a short time after, so he always appreciated that from them.

Sure enough, a couple of hours later after he woke up from his nap, he saw Dad's tablet with a full page of typed information. Dad was not around, but Mom was napping on her cot. Reggie took advantage of this opportunity to read what Dad typed. Yep, it was the doctor's info that Dad wanted him to see. Basically, what it said was that the brain was part of the nervous system that controlled every movement, thought, and feeling experienced on a daily basis. It turned out Reggie's cerebellum had been knocked around a little bit and he was having trouble with language and memory right now.

The doctors were worried about the fact that he was unable to understand signs, but they chalked it up to the trauma of the car sideswiping him. Interestingly, he was able to talk and that was due to the left half of the cerebrum being unaffected. He also was able to write since his hands were partly healed. The right half was what controlled his signing, in their theory. They did not see any damaged neurons in his spinal cord so he was able to wiggle his toes and move his legs around a little.

Another part of his brain that was affected was the limbic system which controlled memories. This was a big part of why he was not remembering signs. But they were at a loss to explain why he was not signing nor understanding signs. They did have a theory after one doctor checked the latest research from Gallaudet University. It turned out that the brain tissue in the auditory cortex, responsible for processing sound, also was responsible for both signed and spoken languages!

There was a new study by a very esteemed doctor at the National Institute of Health with revolutionary findings about the brain and language. Even though sign language had been deemed as equal to spoken language over the past four decades, it was still a huge surprise that the auditory cortex handled sign language in addition to speech and hearing. There had been a huge impact point on the back of Reggie's head from when he fell and hit the cement after the car hit him. The theory from the doctors was that this impact affected the auditory cortex and caused him to forget ASL.

After reading this, he sat back and felt drained. Was he actually doomed to never sign again? He strained to remember any signs that he had used effortlessly his entire life. Yet, he was unable to do so. How frustrating. The tables were turned. His parents were fluent in ASL and he only knew one sign. Laughing, Reggie realized he knew as many signs as Dr. Elizabeth Zinser who had been president of Gallaudet for exactly four days until she was forced to resign as a result of Deaf President Now in 1988. He knew people who had been a part of that protest and he had read _Fighting the Long Sorrow_ which continued to be a favorite book of his that he recommended to all of his classes.

Oh. My. God. What was he going to do about work? He could not fathom teaching in this state of "ASL amnesia". He realized that Sara would get people to cover his classes for the remainder of the fall semester. All of them probably had taught ASL 1 before, but what about the spring? It was only a couple of months away, as it was now nearing the end of October. A thought came into his mind. He should call Sorenson and ask them to install a temporary VideoPhone in his hospital room with a small monitor like the one he had at work. CaptionCall was another option, as it did not require that he know any ASL. All he had to do was talk into the phone and read the captions on the screen when the other person talked.

The next time Dad came back, Reggie asked him to look for Sorenson's phone number for customer service and see if they could bring a VideoPhone. Also, he asked Dad to dig up CaptionCall's contact information. Once that was done, he had nothing else to do except sit up in his bed and watch television.

Those talk shows were becoming addictive, such as Jerry Springer, Maury (always covering "who's the father of my child?"), and Steve Wilkos. The drama on those shows was unbelievable and they were all captioned so he was able to enjoy watching those along with everyone else.

In a few days, he was able to get out of bed and shuffle around although it was painful at times. Luckily, his legs had not been crushed nor broken from the accident so the doctors and his parents were very relieved. Imagine how Reggie felt! The saying about cats having nine lives? He felt like he'd been given a second chance. His left wrist was curled up which was a definite sign of neurological damage and he was doing physical therapy every day on both legs and his right arm. Seeing that his left arm was broken, there was no point in doing therapy on that just yet.

Someone in a white coat came into his room one morning with his parents. Reggie suddenly became nervous, but the calm expressions on his parents' faces relaxed him. It turned out that the doctor wanted to interview him and assess his comprehension about the world around him. Reggie took a deep breath and sat back on the bed, making himself comfortable. Luckily, he could lipread and the ASL interpreter would have been worse than useless.

"Hello, Reggie. I will talk slower than I usually do. My name is Doctor Shapiro and your parents wanted me to ask you some questions. At the same time, I wanted to observe your physical reactions and movements during our conversation. Would that be all right?" He seemed like a very nice man and Reggie felt comfortable with him there, for some reason. He probably got an A+ in medical school for bedside manner!

Shapiro reminded Reggie of that character on "ER". What was his name? Yes, Dr. Marc Greene! He was of average height, was slightly balding, and had rimmed silver glasses. He was not physically imposing and he seemed like a friendly person with his constant smile. Reggie felt okay with him immediately and he was even easy to lipread because he had no facial hair. He suddenly remembered the Latin teacher he'd had in high school with that Santa-like mustache and beard. It had been so bad that Reggie had asked him to trim it that very night after the first day of school even though he'd heard from classmates that the teacher had never trimmed it in years.

Reggie nodded and motioned for Dr. Shapiro to go ahead. Reggie was impatient to get this over with, as he wanted to relax and start trying to remember all of the signs that he had forgotten. He moved around on his bed trying to get into the perfect position, as he still felt a bit awkward in that hospital gown. Whoever designed them was not so smart, as there was that infamous "gap" in the back!

Dr. Shapiro smiled at Reggie and smoothed his tie. "Reggie, where are you?"

Easy question! "I am in Las Vegas somewhere, in a hospital."

The smile grew wider on the doctor's face. "Very good! Who is president of the United States right now?"

Reggie hesitated and had to think for a moment. Hazy faces appeared in his mind. Wasn't it Clinton? "Bill Clinton! He is such a good president, no matter what he did with that girl, what's her name..."

Dr. Shapiro sat there on the edge of his chair, nonplussed. Bill Clinton? This was 2011. That injury definitely had done some serious damage in Reggie Kelleher's brain. Not only was he unable to sign, but he was forgetting such an important and basic piece of information. Everyone knew Barack Obama was President of the United States today! He had seen this before many times in patients who suffered from partial amnesia especially soldiers who were hit by fragments from a IED in Afghanistan or Iraq. But it was important to stay calm and not aggravate a patient.

"Do you know your parents' names?" Another easy question that Reggie should be able to answer with no problem. Dr. Shapiro held his breath and forced his hands not to tremble. He hated to see a patient lose the capacity to remember.

"Max . . . well, is that it? Yes! Maxwell and . . ." Reggie's face twisted in concentration. He seemed to be lost in thought. Dr. Shapiro remained quiet and gave him some more time to think. "Vivian?" Reggie looked up at him with an expectant look on his face.

Dr. Shapiro started to get up. This was a good omen, if Reggie could remember all of these details. He would recover from it eventually, with therapy and time. He walked a few steps over to Reggie and smacked his hand for a high-five. He did not want to overwhelm Reggie at this point. Sensing someone in the doorway behind him, he turned around and saw this attractive woman who had been listening the whole time intently.

He couldn't believe his ears when this woman exclaimed, "Doesn't this hospital have any ASL interpreters on staff? It is illegal not to provide a deaf patient with an interpreter!" She looked very upset and she was signing at the same time, with exaggerated and fast movements. Dr. Shapiro felt uncomfortable and really wanted to leave right there. He refused to even look at her and pointed to Reggie's parents.

"Ma'am, please talk to his parents. They will explain everything." The legal ramifications! He knew that there had been lawsuits against many hospitals in the past including one instance that had shocked him when he googled the issue of

ASL interpreters. That particular incident was when a hearing pregnant woman gave birth and had to interpret for her deaf husband in the delivery room. The hospital was found liable and had to pay hundreds of thousands of dollars in damages. How ridiculous was it that a hospital would deny an interpreter these days!

"Hello, I am done for now. You can come in and visit." He excused himself and hurried out of the room. There were many patients to go see and then he had to supervise residents during their rounds. Never a dull moment!

Chapter 15

Reggie had been just ready to put himself into the routine of daily maintenance with meals, physical therapy, and his parents' being there in the room. Then, suddenly, he noticed someone standing at the doorway. She looked so familiar. Frustrated, he tried to grasp her name. Was it someone he worked with? Yes! It was Sara! He immediately smiled at this unexpected surprise.

Now was a good time as any to start his rehabilitation. Reggie had taken a peek online earlier and saw some of the negative feedback that he got on there including a student who remarked that he thought he was God in the classroom. That told Reggie that he was the type of professor who looked down on students. He didn't want that to happen ever again. He had practically memorized some of the other not-so-nice comments about his teaching style such as:

"Our professor, who we call 'Rego' behind his back due to his huge ego and disdainful attitude, is one of those teachers who has no place being a professor anywhere especially at LVCC. He cannot get his act together. He is very dull and patronizing. Sad excuse for a teacher, period!"

"He gets his jolly good fun from making his tests impossible to pass. It is like a rat's maze where you never find the cheese. This guy is worse in management than George Bush!"

"Rego never cared about my grade for the course. That's why we call him 'REGO' as his ego is bigger than anything I've seen. I have no way of proving what grade I actually got. The worst teacher in LVCC history!"

Ouch. Double Ouch. Triple Ouch. Reggie had to tear his eyes away from these comments. Had he actually been nice to Sara all these years? Or had he been the same way with her that he was with his students? His memory was blurred so he couldn't remember. These grievances were something that was only vaguely present in his mind. It scared him that he was unable to remember them other than just a few details. He could remember sitting in front of the Dean and explaining his side of the situation which was a sad state of affairs. Reprimands had been put in his file and he was warned that if this happened one more time, he could be detenured and ultimately fired.

"Sara . . . how nice of you to come!" Reggie saw her take off her long checkered coat. His eyes slowly widened as he realized what she was wearing. She looked positively radiant in that dress. Actually, she was beyond gorgeous. If he had passed her on the street, he would have stopped in his tracks and done a 180 degree turn to admire the view. Her blouse top revealed some of her cleavage and left little to the imagination. She had black boots on and he could feel them clicking on the floor somehow.

She was surely a vision right now! Reggie swore to himself that he'd never seen her wear a dress before, but today she looked very pretty. Her blouse was a light yellow and it complemented her face really well. The skirt was flowery and she even had makeup on. Had she had a total transformation? Memory or not, he had never seen her like this. He felt very ugly in his hospital robe laying on the bed with this vision from heaven standing in the same room as him.

"You really do look good! I don't think I saw you wear a dress in, like, ever!" Reggie didn't care if he was going overboard in his praise of her, as he really did enjoy looking at her wear that kind of attire. She was a gorgeous woman all of a sudden and he realized she had a figure that men would take a second glance at, including him. She had dressed so drab and boring every day he worked with her. She was sure showing a whole new side of her.

Her facial expression softened and the edges of her mouth curled up in a big smile as Reggie complimented her on how great she looked. She seemed shocked that he was making comments like those. Maybe he had in the past, but not like today. It was like his senses had been heightened after the traumatic experience. His sensitive side was showing today.

She had a surprised expression on her face hearing Reggie talk to her without any ASL and then started signing back to him. He knew that she was taken aback by his lack of signing and he held up his right hand as if he were a stop sign crossing guard.

"This is going to sound strange, but I cannot sign at all. Damage to my brain—at least for now. So you are gonna have to talk to me and I will talk back to you. Surprised, aren't ya?"

Reggie did not enjoy watching her take in this unexpected piece of news, as she had never spoken to him before nor had she really ever heard his voice for longer than a couple of minutes. "But, this isn't really my best speech, as my thought processes are a little delayed right now so I will speak slowly and try my best."

Chapter 16

Sara could not believe what she was hearing. Reggie was not able to sign? Her chest felt like someone had thrust a sword into it. She hurt like she never had before. Her heart felt like it was going to fall into a million pieces. Was this going to be a permanent or temporary setback for him? Her mind performed what seemed to be thousands of calculations in just a few seconds. She remained resolute in her determination to help Reggie get back on his own two feet and show him how she felt about him as a man that she was attracted to.

"What can I do to help you right now, Reggie?" How funny was it she was talking to him. Out of habit, she signed also and realized it was moot to be signing because he wasn't understanding a single sign. She was very worried as she had heard his Clinton answer in response to the doctor's question about who was president now. Didn't he remember George W. Bush and Barack Obama? Everyone would be very surprised at seeing this deaf ASL professor not sign at all.

It was going to be a serious problem in the spring. She would have to advocate for him to the dean and other administrators. Luckily, Reggie had been at LVCC long enough to have job security. Their dean, Roya Esfahani, was a very understanding woman. She knew from talking to Dean Esfahani that her first name meant

"Dream" in Persian. Perhaps she would grant Reggie a leave of absence? Not many people knew this, but Roya and Reggie daily battled in Words with Friends so they had a kinship that very few had with her, as she was a tough woman who prided herself on being fair with faculty and students at LVCC.

Sara felt self-conscious being in the same room with Reggie. Making a mental note to call the Dean as soon as she finished this visit, she was not sure what to do now that she was here and saw Reggie. His parents had somehow left without her realizing it. Just as well. She wanted some privacy to sit down with him. Would he be able to understand her without signing? Of course! She thought back to when Reggie chatted with the department members who were hearing and did not sign. He did just fine with them!

She looked out through the doorway and could see his parents talking with that doctor, serious expressions on their faces. They were probably fixated on that one wrong answer about Clinton. It was something to worry about, but she wanted to get past that for now. At least he was alive, sitting up in bed, and smiling at her. She loved it when Reggie was happy. He did seem very glad to see her. Did he really remember who she was or was he being nice? Only one way to find out.

Smiling awkwardly, her hand weaved through her hair. She walked over to him and looked down at him with a gentle look on her face. She wanted him to feel comfortable around her even if he knew who she was. She pulled up the chair and sat down so their faces were at the same eye level. Time to see if he really knew who she was. She was so nervous and flustered. This was a new feeling for her. If it were almost anyone else, she would not really care that much.

As their eyes locked, she could feel something stirring inside of her. This was a totally new feeling that she had never felt before. Why here and now? She realized it was because Reggie, underneath all that tough exterior and posturing, was really a gentle man who was so funny and endearing to her. Why hadn't anyone snatched him up other than this Pamela that he was living with right now? In fact, where the heck was she? Hello, her boyfriend was in the hospital. She knew that if she were his girlfriend instead of Pamela, she would practically be living at the hospital, spurring Reggie on to full recovery!

She could overhear what the doctor was telling his parents. He was explaining why he couldn't remember Obama or Bush. He had post-traumatic amnesia which was a temporary confusion about the world around him. This would fade away eventually and probably sooner than later. The second type of amnesia which was of paramount concern was the retrograde amnesia which was connected to the auditory cortex. This was why he was unable to remember signs. His voice droned on and on and she didn't want to listen to any more of what he was saying. It was becoming too depressing. She wanted to stay positive and focus on him.

While she was not a religious person per se, she had thanked God for saving Reggie's life. He could easily have died because of that car hitting him. When she heard it on the news, her first thought had been that he was dead and she was never going to see him again. She made a vow to help him learn signs all over again. She needed him both as a colleague and as a possible love interest. Would Reggie be the same person she had known in all those years at LVCC? How soon could he learn the signs that he forgot? An idea came to her.

"Hi, Reggie. I hope you remember me, do you?" She really did hope he remembered her. She made sure she spoke more slowly than normal so he would not have any trouble understanding her. The world seemed to stop as soon as she finished asking the question. So much was riding on this for her.

Chapter 17

What a dumb question that was, Reggie thought. Of course he remembered her! Who could forget Sara Zaslow? This was his ASL colleague and someone like that he could never forget. "Yes, of course I remember you, Sara! Sharing that office, we've had our fun moments. You have been so good to me as a mentor."

It was becoming difficult to pay attention to Sara at this point, as she was really looking spectacular in this dress and wearing those boots. Reggie forced his eyes to stay above her neck, as she looked at him with those piercing eyes. He could feel some kind of connection that he had never really felt before. Was this just his overactive imagination again? Or was there something that had just been ignited when the "moment" happened? He shrugged it off. There was no possible way that a beautiful hearing woman who was ASL fluent would be interested in this brain-damaged guy in a suit that was open on the back! Whoever designed those hospital gowns should be shot and then shot again!

He saw her grinning from ear to ear, as if she were relieved about something that had been on her mind. He could not blame her. She probably had been worried he would have forgotten who she was like he had forgotten all of his ASL. It was so good of her to come visit him in the hospital. She was turning out to be a true friend who cared about him.

Reggie allowed his mind to drift back to Pamela. Why wasn't she coming to the hospital to see him? He felt that she had never really cared about him as a person. She definitely had to know where he was and what had happened. Dad had texted her to let her know what was going on. Reggie was very disappointed in her. This was definitely going to be the end of him and Pamela. It was a long time coming.

He forced himself to return to the present. He would reminisce later. There was a time and a place for that. Not now. Sara gave him a thumbs up. Her face softened as she was about to speak. She seemed to concentrate on talking a bit slower than normal. Reggie knew she had been doing this for many years, as she had worked with deaf people of all ages. Some of them did not sign so she was used to it like his parents were.

"Reggie, I had an idea. It might be too soon to bring it up, and hopefully you will remember your signs before long, but I am gonna throw it out on the table so you can think about it, OK? Remember, I want you to be able to continue working at LVCC. I plan to advocate for you with Dean Roya Esfahani. Let me say her last name again, slowly. Esfahani. Want me to get a piece of paper and write it down? Do you remember Roya?" She hesitated and when Reggie nodded, she continued. "I know you would have trouble lipreading her last name . . ."

Stunned, Reggie gave her his undivided attention as she outlined what she had been thinking about and her thoughts about Roya, who knew him pretty well by now. The plan was that if he did not remember signs when January came around, she would switch places with him and take over all of his ASL classes. The ASL 2 sections would be assigned to adjuncts. Luckily, LVCC had a few great people that were more than able to teach the ASL classes there. She also said he could take over the lab with very little training. The aides would help him out and there was just organization to do as well as orientations that he could give out the first couple of weeks in January.

That really did sound doable. He knew how lucky he had been, escaping any serious, fatal injury and nothing was permanent. Over time, he probably would recover. But he was very nervous about the fact that he was unable to sign right now. Sara was going overboard in making sure he had a place at LVCC and her willingness to switch places with him did touch him deep inside his heart. He knew this could not be easy for her, but she was going the extra mile for him. Reggie now really felt the pull to divulge his attraction to Sara right there and then.

It was a good thing he could speak and lipread well! "Sara, you are amazing. Thank you for going the distance with me. You really can understand me that well?"

His feelings for her were growing leaps and bounds by the minute and second. Why had he never been in touch with his feelings before? It was like he had built a wall around his heart with everyone except his parents. Seeing her nod in response to his question, he was unable to restrain himself any more. Everything seemed to be moving in slow motion. His mind quickly pictured all of the hearing and deaf women who he had been with. Nobody could hold a candle to Sara except maybe Angie. But he had lost touch with Angie and he had not been able to find her on Facebook at all. It was time to look ahead.

"Can I have a hug, Sara? I feel overwhelmed right now by your generosity and support!" After the traumatic few days he'd had, he really needed a hug from her. It was different coming from Mom and Dad. This was someone who had no obligation to be here for her. Parents were one thing, a friend and colleague another.

She enveloped him into the best hug he'd ever had. He buried his head in her hair. What was that smell? Lavender, his favorite! She made him feel safe and important. Very few people could do that for him. He whispered into her ear, "You are the best, Sara. I am going to say something important that I've not been brave enough to tell you before. I am just happy I am still alive and have this second chance on earth to share with you . . ."

Sara gently pushed him away from her and her eyes bore into his. He could see her eyes glistening and he realized she was almost crying! Gathering his strength, he vowed not to lose his resolve. "You are very important to me, Sara. I have been holding back on you . . ."

Her face became one of confusion and concern. With eyebrows up, her head tilted to the side. Reggie hurried to make her feel at ease. "What I meant, Sara, is that I have strong feelings for you . . ."

It was the God-honest truth. How had he been so blind all this time with her sitting in their office, sharing many jokes and war stories from their teaching careers? For a few months, he had joined a local gym that Sara belonged to. Often, when he was there, she had come by to work out and she even gave him some pointers! He could not remember one instance where he had been unhappy around her. He could not believe that he had overlooked this vision of beauty and he silently thanked God that she was not married yet. What about that boyfriend of hers? Ignoring that reality, he spurred himself to continue or the moment would be lost forever.

"In fact, I was running to a neighbor's house to call Dad and arrange for the ball to get rolling on my breakup with Pamela. I wanted to start a new life without her so I could eventually ask you out on a real date once I was brave enough. But . . . you have a boyfriend so I know I cannot do that yet. Whew, I cannot believe I am being so forthcoming. But I almost never had this opportunity!"

Sara stood there, arms at her sides. Her mouth dropped open and she was not moving at all. Then, slowly, as if realization dawned on her, she started to smile. Hesitatingly at first, but in a few seconds, she was grinning with tears streaking down her face. "Are you serious, Reggie? You have these feelings for me?"

"What can I say, Sara? I've always had a thing for you! I just didn't realize it before. Do you have the same feelings for me?" He held out hope that she in fact did and he would no longer feel alone in this world in terms of affection, love, romance, and companionship. He braced himself for rejection and humiliation if she said no to him.

She nodded and walked towards him again, enveloping him in another hug. Her lips gently touched his. To him, her lips felt perfect! Fireworks exploded inside his head. So tender, soft, warm! It all finally came together and felt perfect to him. Sara Zaslow was in love with him just like he was with her! The universe finally made sense. Reggie was so happy, elated, and excited.

The minutes felt like hours. He wanted to savor this moment for as long as he could. The speech therapy and ASL tutoring would be unrelenting for him in the upcoming days, weeks, and months. He wanted to get back to ASL fluency so he could return to the classroom with his brand-new persona. He knew students would not believe it at first and he could not wait to see their expressions when they encountered a positive, happy, radiant Reggie Kelleher. No more Rego!

Finally, the kiss ended and her face was just inches from his. "Reggie, don't worry . . ." She was really easy to lipread so she did not have to sign. She uttered each word slowly and clearly for him to understand without much effort. "I am going to be there for you. Just promise me one thing, please."

He couldn't imagine what that one thing was that Sara wanted from him. Was it his undying love for her? Shouting it from the rooftops? He very much doubted it.

"What is it? You know I'll do anything, pretty much."

"Reggie, I want you to start coming to my ASL 101 classes and give it all you have. You can shadow me in one or two 101 sections in the spring and start from scratch. For now, come to one of your current sections. How about the one that is the first class of the day on Monday? Lindsay was actually here to check on your progress and I ran into her in the lobby. You remember L-I-N-D-S-A-Y? Whatever works for you. Don't be embarrassed by learning all over again. Maybe one day everything will pop back into your mind and you can teach your classes. I will give your classes to some of the adjuncts who can finish your semester. You can consult with them about tests, lesson plans, etc. I can interpret for you with the two deaf adjuncts. OK?"

Reggie thought that wasn't so bad. "Sounds good, Sara—I can do that! When can I start coming to your class next week? How about the early one that I used to teach? You can take over that class, right? I know all of the adjuncts work in the mornings at one job or another so it will be tough to cover."

Sara nodded and it looked like a done deal. That was going to be weird, the infamous Reggie Kelleher taking the same class as those students who made a bet on him at the beginning of the semester. He wondered how she would handle this group and he wondered how she would teach that specific class because their attitude had been rotten with him. Then, he realized that the only reason they had that attitude was because of him! That very thought was enough to make him feel more humble and contrite.

Plus, those students voiced a lot and with a hearing teacher, they couldn't do that anymore. He felt relieved that all the pressure was off him. It made for a very nice evening, as Sara stayed for a while to chat with him. She even hopped onto his bed and snuggled with him for a bit before leaving. How had he gotten so lucky with her having the same feelings?

Finally, it came time for her to leave and she seemed very reluctant to do so. Reggie felt panicky. He wanted her to stay with him every day and night. But he likely was going home soon, although it would be with his parents and not Pamela, so it would not be long before he would see her every day at work again. He was really looking forward to being at LVCC again, but he knew the doctors wanted him to take it easy for a while.

"Sara, see you Monday morning bright and early! Remember, that class you have first thing voices a lot so I am glad you will be teaching it. I am going to be a star student for you!" Laughing, he signed YES which was half of the vocabulary he had at that point, with the only other sign he knew being NO.

What was Sara doing? That sign phrase looked familiar. She first pointed at herself in the chest, then crossed her arms on the chest, and pointed at him. He knew it meant something important and there was a fuzzy part of his brain where he could not grasp the meaning. So frustrating! It was just barely out of his reach.

"I know that means something really important, but I am sorry . . ." He felt like a total idiot for not being able to remember this phrase. It was a given she was going to turn around and leave in a huff. He felt so small at that very moment.

"Reggie, don't be silly. It means 'I love you' and I really do! I had not realized it before but I've felt this way for a while. I am just happy you are alive and well for me to share my life with. Let's make the most of second chances."

He felt so much relief at her unconditional acceptance. Waving, she walked out of the hospital room and she looked back one more time, blowing him a kiss. He made the gesture of catching it with both hands and kissing his palms. She laughed, shook her hand, and waved the 'ILY' sign as she disappeared down the hallway to the elevator.

Invigorated, he sat up in bed and grabbed a pad of paper along with a pen. Concentrating hard, he started writing his dating history so he could share it with Sara the next time they got together. He wanted her to understand the ups and downs that he'd had with women especially the mistakes they'd made such as leaving him out of conversations and talking on cell phones without telling him who they were talking to. In fact, one of his girlfriends who did that later confessed it was a hearing man that she had been cheating with behind his back. He shuddered and considered himself lucky to be done with a woman like that.

Chapter 18

The weekend was over before Reggie knew it. The discharge from the hospital had gone smoothly and he had gotten an admonishment from Dr. Shapiro to really watch himself for the first few weeks at LVCC. Reggie was actually sorry to say goodbye to Dr. Shapiro who had been very patient and kind with him. He wished all doctors were like that. He knew he would be going back to the hospital outpatient wing for physical therapy for a while. Never had he worked so hard at such basic movements. His broken arm was mending and the cast would be coming off in a few more weeks.

He was back home at his parents' on Monday morning. Breakfast was his usual staple of Cheerios and Fiber One with Silk unsweetened milk and it was delicious. He even added some Honey O's on top of it for more flavor. He was very nervous going back to class even though he was not teaching for the rest of the semester. Just to see Sara again! Was last Friday a dream or his imagination? Or did it really happen? He looked at the pad next to his bowl of cereal and he had already written over ten pages in it about his dating history. He was very careful about keeping it private, as there were things in it that would cause him embarrassment if anyone other than Sara saw it.

His iPhone buzzed on the table as he was putting another spoonful of cereal in his mouth. HEY REGGIE, SEE YOU IN A FEW! ALREADY AT LVCC. LOVE YOU! LAST WK NOT A MIRAGE! XO SARA. Reggie smiled broadly and thought about her. She knew him so well that she actually had thought he would question whether their rendezvous had really happened. What a smart lady Sara was! What would it be like having a lover and friend in the same office? Maybe it would not be so bad. He had heard of office romances and this definitely qualified as one!

It was a very quick drive to LVCC. There was usually little traffic at the pre-dawn hour and he parked on campus. He could even see the house where Pamela was sleeping. That was something he needed to take care of soon. It was seared onto his brain and he had thought about it all weekend. It was time to let the realty company know that he was moving out and she was to be evicted. Where she went was no concern of his. She had blown it with her uncaring attitude towards him over the past weeks when he was hospitalized.

How had he been so blind for so long? The difference in how Sara treated him was so different from Pamela. He had not gotten even a peep from Pamela. No texts, no calls, not even a short visit. Was this how Pamela felt about him? It was not like she had to worry about kids, pets, or even working too much. She had no excuse for not visiting and watching over him. As far as he was concerned, that was done, over with, kaput, finished! This was all in the notes that he wrote on the pad that weekend. He was ready to share so many secrets with Sara.

Bypassing his office, he walked to class. There was not enough time to check his inbox which he knew from Sara would be full of cards, memos, and everything else. It would take too long to go through. Taking a deep breath, he stopped at the doorway of the classroom and did a double-take. There was a huge banner above the doorway that said "WELCOME BACK, PROF. KELLEHER!"

Reggie was stunned and had not expected that. There were balloons tied to both ends of the banner right outside the doorway. Opening the door slowly, his eyes landed on each of the students sitting in the room. He hesitatingly stepped inside and took a look around the semicircle of seated students.

All conversation stopped and everyone looked in his direction. He waved and felt very self-conscious. The students all smiled and waved their hands in the air. He suddenly felt at ease. What had he done to deserve such kindness from a class that he had been especially mean to all semester? He had never felt so much guilt in his life. He remembered suddenly the life review that he'd had when he felt all of the emotions that the students felt with his scathing rebukes and disdainful attitude. He silently vowed to make it up to them over the rest of the semester and in the spring. Knowing that voice was not allowed in the classroom, he shrugged and went for an empty desk right near the doorway in case he needed to get out of the room for whatever reason.

In the hospital, he had mulled over the way he treated these students. He had been very callous, snotty, and demeaning. Now he was going to be in their shoes and knew he had to do well with learning ASL in order to keep his job at LVCC. He knew he would learn quickly. Ah, there was Lindsay in her usual seat. He looked at her, mouthing "Thank you for checking on me at the hospital!" She nodded back at him with a friendly look on her face as Sara walked into the classroom and plopped her bag on the desk. Reggie inwardly smiled, but kept his poker face and looked away quickly.

Then, Reggie realized what he was doing just like he had done before his accident. He was trivializing how his students had felt and this was a bad habit that he'd vowed to get rid of. He immediately erased the thought from his mind and put it aside. Lindsay was a sweet girl and she was always nice to him in spite of everything. Reggie's head turned back to Lindsay and nodded. He could see what a difference it made, as her face lit up immediately. It was time to focus on Sara who was the professor in his shoes. He could see that Sara took a quick look around and when her eyes were on him, she smiled with a nod in his direction.

Reggie continued to look at her and braced himself for a hour and fifteen minutes of humble pie. He was now officially on the other end of the classroom. Where were they in the workbook? Ah, the autobiography on page 90! It did seem very familiar and Sara motioned for people to break up into groups to practice for their presentations which were coming up soon. He willed himself not to panic and told himself to just go with the flow.

He made sure he joined Lindsay's group, as she was really nice. She had been one of his favorite students with such a positive attitude. He moved his desk over to where she was sitting with three other students on the opposite side of the room. He quickly checked his notebook to make sure the pad of paper, now folded in half, was still in his workbook.

Now he was unable to communicate with anyone so he just sat there watching as the four students in the group took turns signing their autobiographies. Lindsay sat next to him and pointed to where each student was signing. After a while, he got the hang of the vocabulary and realized for time transition between different periods, he was supposed to raise his eyebrows. There were four time periods in the autobiography: growing up, high school, college, and now. That seemed easy enough.

The vocabulary started to come easily to him. He picked up the signs quickly and remembered them the first time he saw each sign. Some students had to repeat the autobiography several times, but it only took him one run-through to get it all perfectly. Lindsay and the others in the group looked surprised. He could not sign what he did not know, so he tore a piece of paper from his notebook and wrote, 'IT IS LIKE RIDING A BIKE! COMING BACK TO ME SLOWLY, BUT SURELY!' Lindsay chuckled and passed it around to each group member.

Sara was walking around the classroom and then she came over to them. She looked at Reggie questioningly and he gave her a reassuring nod, pointing at Lindsay. He motioned a thumbs-up and Sara seemed satisfied, watching the students sign their stories. It was then he knew everything would be all right.

Chapter 19

Max Kelleher sat in his office, seething about the thought that Rocks had been the person who hit his son on the sidewalk and had almost killed him. Just to think he had tried to warn Reggie at the Luxor Hotel not too long ago! The phone rang and he took a look at the Caller I.D. to see who was calling him. It was the police department! Maybe there had been a break in the hit-and-run. He had high hopes that someone had seen something. He knew that Rocks was not stupid enough to use his real name renting a car or using his own vehicle.

"What did you say?" He was incredulous, just finding out that Rocks was dead. His car had hit an oak tree in one of the Vegas suburbs just now, a few blocks away from where Reggie had been hit. "He's dead? Are you absolutely sure? Okay, thank you for letting me know about this. Just incredible!" He slowly put the receiver back down on the phone and he didn't know what to think right now. First, his son had been hit by a car driven by an old nemesis and now that nemesis was dead. He had not called the police department since the accident happened. He wanted to focus on Reggie who was in the hospital. Luckily, the injuries had not been serious and Reggie was now at home with him and his wife so they could keep an eye on him.

It was time to face the Family one more time to wrap things up and maybe even get an official apology from the consigliere who was Rocks' boss. Maybe they would call off the dogs and let them live their lives. The Kellehers did not need to keep watching over their shoulders every day. Hiring bodyguards would be so expensive, kind of like having the Secret Service 24/7. Only rich Hollywood stars and megamillionaire sports players could afford this kind of service.

He flipped through his Rolodex and looked for his contacts who still worked in the Family. It was funny how he still used a Rolodex. People made fun of it, but he stuck to what worked. It was like Theresa Caputo and her cassette player which was practically an antique. It worked great for her so why shouldn't he do what came naturally for him also? Who cares what people said about the Rolodex. If it worked for him, so be it. Reggie had seen it and always got a good laugh out of that. He smiled at the memory and it made him more determined to make sure his whole family was secure from the Family.

Ah, here it is. Ballardi, Salvatore. Also known as Sal the Pal. He was a very popular figure in the Family and everyone in Vegas knew who he was. His office was right near the Luxor Hotel, in a really opulent building. It reminded him of the Bellagio which was further north on the Strip with those fountains. Taking a deep breath, his hands trying not to shake, he picked up the phone receiver and dialed the number. The phone rang at the other end and after three rings, someone answered.

"Yes, this is the operator for Ballardi Industries. May I help you?"

Max recognized the voice. It was Della. Nobody knew her last name, but she was practically an institution at the company, having worked there for many years. She was absolutely discreet and very reliable. Della had never married so she was an ideal person to be the receptionist there. She went home every day to an empty apartment and never spoke to anyone about what went on at work. She had very few friends, but she was well-liked by the executives and other employees at B.I.

"Hi, Della! This is Max Kelleher. Is Sal in now?" He could imagine the reaction from Della upon hearing his voice on the phone.

He was not disappointed. "Max! What a nice surprise! It has been a long time. Yes, Sal is here in his office. Let me connect you. Oh, by the way, I am sorry to hear about Reggie. Hope he will recover completely and be able to go back to work."

Max was not surprised. Della was a really kind person who always asked about his wife and son when he had worked with Ballardi Industries in various capacities. "Thank you so much, Della. I appreciate that. Hope you are doing well yourself. It is amazing that you are still there, but it is comforting to hear your voice!"

He could practically sense Della's smile through the phone as if that were possible. Waiting with bated breath for Sal to answer, he looked at his watch and tapped his fingers on the desk. Patience, man. For someone like Sal, you waited as long as it took. No matter what. No complaining. Unless you wanted to sleep with the fish and wear cement shoes!

"Max! How are you, old friend and colleague?" The booming voice of Sal the Pal could not be more distinct. Max would know that voice from anywhere. He was always boisterous and loud any time he spoke with Sal.

"I am better now than before, thank you. Reggie is doing much better. That's why I wanted to talk to you. About something that concerns me a great deal." Nothing better than to get straight to the point. No bullshitting around. He was like Reggie in that regard. He knew that was a characteristic of many deaf people, being blunt and direct.

A lot of people did not like that about Max, but that was how he did business with anyone. It was nothing personal. Sal the Pal was the same way. That was one major reason they got along so well as business partners in the past. They had done many business deals together and sometimes the transactions had not exactly been legal, but nobody found out due to their mutual assurances of staying quiet about all of it. Never had either of them betrayed the other. Thus, they had a high regard for each other as business equals.

Sal the Pal was mystified. Why was Max calling him after so many years of not staying in touch? Was it connected to his son? If so, what could it possibly be? He sat there patiently, reclining his chair back in comfort. His eyes closed and he could remember the circumstances that had brought him in contact with Max all those years ago at the Luxor Hotel.

Sal was not even supposed to be in Vegas that day, but someone else in the Family had gotten sick so he was sent in the other person's place to meet this Maxwell Kelleher, an up-and-coming executive at this store in the Luxor. It had been a fortuitous meeting and they had many business deals together after that. He liked Max a great deal and thought it was a shame how the Family had treated Max by cutting off all ties with him.

Sal himself was not really a good looking guy. He reminded many people of Tony Soprano. He was heavy, not-so-tall, and had thick, black hair (unlike the Soprano character who was going bald). He was definitely not seeing a therapist either. To him, that signified weakness and it had been a sore point for him when HBO portrayed that part of the character on-screen. He made sure everyone knew how he felt about that. He always dressed in suits with the latest designs. He never scrimped on what he wore every day. Even on the weekends, he was dressed for business. In his mind, he was always ready to go at a moment's notice.

Finally, he heard Max's voice. "Sal, it has to do with the hit and run. You know, it has been on the news, but the police are keeping quiet about the investigation. But I know who the driver was. A business associate of yours who just got out of prison." No way! He realized now what the connection was: Rocchino.

"I feel terrible, Max. Didn't realize that Rocks was gunning for your son. There is no connection with me or Ballard Industries. I give you my solemn word on that. No harm will come to you, your wife, and your son from now on. I will put the word out to stay away from you, honoring our previous agreement. I never knew about Rocks, my friend!" He felt really terrible, but that was the nature of the job that Max had been involved with before. It could happen to anyone, basically.

"Max, an afterthought. This is why I live in a gated community here on the outskirts of Vegas. It has 24 hour security with a manned gate at all times. There is no way anyone can come after me when I am home. My villa has its own elevator which allows me to park in the garage and come upstairs without exposing myself outside. You might want to do the same thing from now on."

Max listened as Sal droned on about the complex he lived in. That was not a bad idea at all. Communities like that were sprouting all over after the housing slump had hit bottom a year or two ago. Prices were starting to rebound. He really should think about moving into a more secure environment.

"Sal, thank you for the great suggestion. I am going to talk to my wife. I am very relieved you had nothing to do with this hit and run. So, we are on good terms and have nothing to worry about from the Family?"

"Absolutely nothing to worry about, Max. You are safe and never need to look over your shoulder again. As a sign of public respect, I will contact the several communities to give you a tour of their grounds so you can get an idea what this kind of living is like for us. If anyone goes after you, he will be dealt with harshly. I truly am sorry for your emotional and mental anguish. I can only imagine how I'd feel if that had happened to me like that."

It looked like this had been a personal vendetta, nothing to do with his past with the Family. That was a very good thing and a matter of great relief for Max. Now he did not feel guilty anymore and could face his wife and son again. He had struggled internally when looking at Reggie on his bed with tubes all over him. It reminded him of what his own father had looked like near the end of his life after the massive heart attack. He had passed away only a few days after the last coronary and Max had never gotten the chance to say goodbye.

"Thanks, Sal. I will not forget this and please do let me know about the different complexes. Maybe you can get me a good deal at one of them!"

"Absolutely! I will reach out and then get back to you, old friend. You take care and please send my regards to everyone. Also, I am going to do you a huge favor. I am not going to reveal what that is just yet, but if the situation arises, you will find out what it is. It could possibly be the best thing that anyone ever did for you!"

Max gently placed the receiver back on the phone and exhaled. That had not been so bad after all. What did Sal the Pal mean with that last comment about the favor? Whatever it was, there was nothing threatening him or his family. He felt a huge weight being lifted off his shoulders and he had not felt this good in weeks. He could not wait to go home and tell Vivian the news that they were safe. He also wanted to look into the communities once he heard back from Sal. He had friends in New York, Florida, and Arizona who lived at communities like that. They all loved it especially the social aspect with classes, workshops, outings, and parties. Nobody felt alone in a complex like that.

He had seen pictures online and they looked amazing. He was not getting any younger and it was time to pamper himself accordingly. Who knows how many years one has left? He felt ready to move on with his life. Maybe Reggie could live with them for awhile. He suddenly realized who the female visitor had been the other day. Wasn't that Sara Zaslow? She worked with his son at LVCC. What a nice woman. Maybe there was a possibility there. Wouldn't that be nice, his son with a hearing woman who was fluent in ASL. He would feel a lot better knowing Reggie was in good hands.

Chapter 20

Sara Zaslow breathed a sigh of relief as she walked to her car after classes ended that day. Reggie had done very well especially for someone who was starting from scratch. But he had been a trooper and was picking up ASL very quickly. He only had to be shown a sign once and it stuck to him like a Post-It note. It really was uncanny. Now he was in the lab watching the entire workbook DVD from "Signing Naturally". Since this was a period of time right after the first lab was already due, the lab was very quiet and it was the perfect time for Reggie to focus on learning ASL. He also took the initiative to subscribe to a great website that featured monthly subscriptions for people who wanted to learn ASL online.

It was time to call Dean Roya Esfahani and explain the situation update. Sara knew her very well. The Dean was a very well-respected person on campus. As a teenager, she had escaped from the Revolution in the 1970's when Shah Reza Pahlavi was removed from office. The fundamentalist revolution started with the Ayatollah Khomeini and the American hostages who were imprisoned for 444 days until Ronald Reagan was inaugurated as president. Roya told her about the rumors that abounded in Iran about George H.W. Bush's working behind the scenes to delay the hostages' release until after the election to ensure that Jimmy Carter lost.

Roya had come to America with her family with no knowledge of English at all. She had to start all over and read kids' books in English, but she learned very quickly and by the time she was in her senior year of high school, she had achieved straight A's to become valedictorian of her graduating class. She continued her stellar performance in college and graduate school at Georgetown University, joining LVCC as a political science professor. She worked her way up the ranks to the current dean position she was in now. She had also been the chair of her department for a few years previously.

Sara was not worried, but she needed to dot the I's and cross the T's just to make sure Reggie was safe with his job at LVCC. Whipping out her iPhone, she went to the directory and dialed Roya's number. After the second ring, she heard someone pick up.

"Hi, this is Sara Zaslow—is this Dean Esfahani? I need to speak to her about something urgent related to one of my colleagues at LVCC." She hoped Roya was answering and not someone else. This really needed to be taken care of quickly. The sooner, the better.

To her relief, the voice was familiar, that of Roya. "Yes, this is Roya. How are you? Done with your classes for the day?"

Sara laughed. "Yes, but I am not used to teaching several sections anymore. I have been cooped up in my office for years at the lab and now I am in front of students again. That's not a bad thing. Don't get me wrong. I am not complaining. It is just different. I had forgotten what it was like to do this several times a day. Reggie has been really great! Did you know he will be coming to my Monday and Wednesday 8 a.m. ASL 101 class until Christmas break and again next semester?"

Roya was surprised, not sure what the reaction would be from Reggie's former students. She wanted to clarify things. "Why is he doing that? Can't he learn all of the signs in the lab without going to classes? I mean, look at Rosetta Stone. People can become really adept in languages on their own, can't they? I do not understand." This was unsettling news and something which she needed to find more information about.

Sara forced herself not to sigh, as Roya would overhear it on the phone. A lot of people did not grasp the notion that ASL was a language that was almost impossible to learn on one's own.

"As you know, Roya, Reggie suffered a serious brain injury as a result of the hit-and-run several weeks ago. As we discussed before, he is back and we have decided to switch places so he can refresh his memory with ASL and connect the dots. Plus, the lab is much less physically demanding for him so he can focus on his recovery with physical therapy and counseling." This was something she really believed would be temporary and she was going to make sure Reggie learned ASL very quickly so he could keep his job as a professor.

Roya pondered and wet her lips in concentration. That sounded reasonable to her. "Fine, that's fine. It sounds doable to me. I appreciate the heads-up about this. Frankly, I was quite worried when you mentioned 'brain injury' and was expecting much worse news, but I was not sure what you would say. I will go to the administration and explain this to them in an update next week."

What a relief that Roya supported her! Now she could hit the ground full-speed ahead and get Reggie back to where he had been. They would have to go to many deaf events and luckily, Thanksgiving was just around the corner. Numerous deaf events were scheduled and she vowed to bring him to as many as possible. She knew that immersion was the biggest open secret of becoming fluent in ASL. She got frustrated when students complained about taking too long to learn ASL. They expected to be fluent after only one semester of classes.

She could remember one day when she had invited Reggie to come visit her ASL 102 class. Knowing Reggie's penchant for being direct, she had warned her students and reminded them of deaf people's bluntness. When he came in, they had first been receptive and asked him questions about learning ASL. Then, he said to them (and she would never forget this), "How many hours have you been learning ASL?"

There had been no movement in the class when he asked that question. His eyebrows arched up and he looked around the room askance. He looked each student in the eyes for a few seconds each and then signed, "Well . . . ?"

She knew her students very well and she could tell they were all surprised at this question. So, she got up off her chair and wrote on the blackboard, using calculations. After a few minutes, she turned around and signed, "You have only been learning ASL for about three days after being in classes for 1 ½ semesters. Don't you all realize that?" The students stared at the math which was undeniable. About thirty six hours of ASL in 101 and now 18 hours in 102.

Reggie raised his eyebrows at them and pointed to the board. "How do you expect to become fluent in ASL by just learning in the classroom? I have met hearing people who went from nothing to fluency in one semester or even less. How was this possible?" Luckily, Sara was voice interpreting for him so they all could understand his point.

Hands shot up. Reggie picked out each student to answer. Unsurprisingly, they were all wrong. They guessed things like using the DVD over and over, getting a tutor, practicing with each other via Skype on Facebook, signing in front of a mirror, using iPhone apps, and other modes. Reggie had chafed at each answer, shaking his head. "You are all wrong. The number one way to learn

ASL, aside from the classroom, is . . ." He paused for dramatic effect and waited for Sara to catch up to him five seconds later.

Once he lipread her saying ". . . aside from the classroom, is . . ." He signed, "IMMERSION!" with exaggerated movements to stress his point. "Let me fingerspell it for you . . . I-M-M-E-R-S-I-O-N! What does that mean? Going to tons of deaf events, making deaf friends, attending interpreted lectures, getting out there in the Deaf world. This is how you learn quickly. Don't dip your feet in the water. Dive in!"

That had not gone over well with her class, but she knew Reggie was 100% correct in stressing immersion. She was going to use him this semester as proof of how to learn ASL by immersion. Laughing, she shook her head at the memory. She had not seen any students go to deaf events after that. Predictably, nobody became fluent from that class. It was very rare that she met a student who became an interpreter unless he or she joined the deaf world and made a total commitment.

Now that Reggie knew no signs, she was going to try to make arrangements to have Reggie videotaped, starting in the next class. That way, she could document it all and an idea just popped into her head. It would make for an interesting documentary about him that she could use for income so they could pay for medical bills and counseling just in case insurance did not cover some of it. Now that was genius!

Her cell phone rang, zapping her out of her reverie. Dazed, she leaned on the driver's side of the car and looked at the display. Oh, no. It was her ex! She had hoped he would not call her back and prolong the misery. What did Marcus Brossler have to say that was supposed to win her back? There was no way that would happen. Or was he just calling to say goodbye? Her bet was on him trying to persuade her to give him another chance. She had given him plenty of chances. The physical marks on her had faded, but it was seared in her mind and heart.

Sighing, she decided not to take the call and typed instead.

IF YOU KEEP CALLING ME, I WILL GO TO THE POLICE. YOU WILL BE SERVED A RESTRAINING ORDER. THIS IS YOUR FIRST AND LAST WARNING. THANK YOU, FROM SARA.

Now that should do the trick. She never wanted to see that jerk again, especially after finding out that Reggie was in love with her. Something about him did haunt her and she was really curious as to what it was. She had good instincts about people's moods and she was very rarely wrong. People told her she was like a psychic, but she was no medium and she never saw lottery numbers! Why is it that psychics said they knew the future, but nobody spoke up before 9/11 and she had never heard of one winning the lottery!

She was definitely worried about Marcus and whether he would show up at home or LVCC. That reminded her. She proceeded to put "911" on her speed-dial right at the very top of the phone directory. Anytime she did not have to use the phone, she vowed to put the cursor right on top of "911" just in case. She also had her Mace spray. While that was not exactly legal, she did not care at the moment. Her safety was paramount.

She shuddered at the memories of being with Marcus. He had slapped her around for no reason, giving her a red mark on her face each time. She had been able to cover those bruises up with makeup, but it was never a good feeling to be treated like that. He also had threatened her, saying he would kill her if she ever broke up with him and he even said he would target the next guy she went out with. She believed him and hoped there was some way to prevent this from happening.

So far, Marcus had not texted her back. That was good. Or it could be very bad, as he might start stalking her and then things would be worse. She decided to text Reggie and see how he was. Maybe she could go visit him and spend some time with him. REG, R U HOME? CAN I COME VISIT? LOVE, SARA. Putting the phone in her purse, she got into her car and made herself comfortable. BUZZ! Was that her phone already? Yes, Reggie had written back! SURE, COME ON OVER. WUD LUV TO C U 2DAY. AT FOLKS' NOW. LOTS TO TELL U. LOVE BACK, XO REG.

Great! Off she went. She knew where Max and Vivian lived. No need for GPS like she usually did. Even though she had lived in Vegas for years, she still needed navigation help to get around. It was not long before she arrived at the Kellehers' house. She was nervous! What if his parents were around and knew what had happened to their relationship? Girding herself, she got out of the car, walked to the front door, and rang the doorbell. Surprised, she saw flashing lights all over the house. That was amazing of his parents to set up an alert system for their son so he would know if someone was at the door. Many of her students at LVCC commented on this type of alarm system in their lab after watching the DVD, "Sign of Respect."

It was only a few seconds before the front door opened and there was Reggie! He had a huge smile on his face. "Welcome, Sara! Come on in. My folks are here also." Then, he whispered into her ear, "Don't worry. Dad already talked about you and praised you to the heavens. You walk on water as far as they're concerned!"

Sara immediately started to relax. This was a good thing. She was going to be just fine with the Kelleher family. It was really incredible how fluent the parents were just for Reggie. She knew over eighty percent of hearing parents who had a deaf child did not sign and that really made her very upset. She talked about that in her classes and students always expressed shock. Some even became angry that parents would deny their deaf children equal access to information like at the dinner table.

She walked into the family room. The Kelleher house was gorgeous and a typical Southwestern home. There was no basement. But the house was all renovated with new appliances and carpet. This kind of home would sell quickly even in the slumping Vegas housing market. They took good care of this place so that was important. The shrubbery and grass outside were immaculate.

"Hello, Mr. and Mrs. Kelleher. Good to see you again!" She was unsure whether to hug them or shake their hand. Of course, Reggie had hugged her. He would have done that even as merely a friend, as deaf culture mandated hugs when friends saw each other again after awhile.

Before she knew it, Max embraced her and said, "Thank you for all you've done for our son!" She could feel him signing behind her back for Reggie to see. "Oh, silly me. This is such a force of habit, signing for my son." He laughed and stepped back to look at Reggie. "I told her thank you for everything. Why am I signing when you don't remember ASL? Maybe if we all keep signing, it will come back to you. Who knows? Sara, please don't be formal with Vivian and me. We are like family now. Capisce?"

Reggie couldn't be happier to see his parents accept Sara like a family member. What they didn't know was that Sara and he were romantically involved and now was the time to divulge that news. Hoping Sara didn't get upset with him, he walked over to her and put his right arm around her shoulder. He then proceeded to kiss her on the cheek and turned to his parents.

"Mom, Dad. Sara doesn't know I am going to share this with you, but we are now together. Not just friends anymore. I am in love with her and she with me!"

Sara did a double-take. That was not part of the plan! But she was happy that Reggie wanted his parents to know what was going on. Now it was official! They were together and nothing could break them apart. Not even Marcus. She would worry about his threats later. She knew she would have to share this information with Reggie. But for now, she had to work on him getting his sign fluency back.

Max and Vivian were delighted at the news. Vivian started to cry and Max wrapped her around with his big arms. "It's OK, dear. Everything will be fine." All of the pressure and drama from the past few weeks seemed to melt away from everyone in this room. Nobody wanted this moment to end, as they felt like kindred spirits with such goodwill and a strong bond between them.

Finally, the spell was broken when Reggie commented, "Sara really saved my job with Dean Roya. I can never pronounce her last name. Isn't it Persian? One of my students from a couple of years ago told me that was a common last name in Iran. Is that right, Dad?" He knew Max was a frequent traveler and a big fan of Travel Channel so if anyone would know, it would be him.

"Absolutely right! If you Google that, you will see that is one of the most common last names there." He smiled at his son and was proud to have such a worldly knowledge of geography. "Wait, let me think. Isn't the DeafWorld Expo coming up soon? Reggie?"

Reggie stared at Dad and he scrambled to think back to the summer. He remembered vaguely having read a flyer on Facebook about this event which was supposed to be huge, only happening once a year in Vegas. Everyone in the deaf community came together to see what new products were out and anything could be hawked such as clothes, services, agencies, businesses, etc. It was a great way to get a pulse on the deaf community annually.

"Dad, you are right—Sara, isn't that in January?" He looked at her in askance. She nodded and signed YES TRUE. Ah, that was going to be kind of tricky if he still did not remember many signs, but they would make the best of it. "Are you guys coming to the Expo also?"

Max and Vivian both nodded and that made him happy. Every year, they had come up with some kind of excuse why they were not going, but not this year. Was it the near-death scare that happened recently? He did not care about the reason. He was thrilled to have his parents at the Expo and Sara also, of course. This was the beginning of a new life. Now he had to "fix" his reputation at LVCC with the students. What was a good way to start doing that?

He motioned to Sara to sit in the family room. Pictures of him were all over the walls. Some alone, some with his parents. He had been embarrassed by these photos growing up, but now he treasured them. Many good memories came back to him as he glanced at each one. Hopefully, they would help him remember his ASL eventually. Sitting down on the sofa, Sara was right next to him. He put his hands on top of hers.

"I know I already thanked you for what you are doing at LVCC for me. I just wanted to ask you to go to DeafWorld with me. I wouldn't want to go with anyone else! Would you do me the honor of that?" Sara nodded slowly. No words needed to be said.

Time went by very quickly. Thanksgiving was a small, intimate affair with just the four of them eating at home, with nobody cooking. They did a catered meal from Boston Market which left them with plenty of time to relax and chat. The usual football game was on and they watched it all together, basking in the atmosphere of love and togetherness.

After Thanksgiving, Pamela was asked to leave the house near LVCC and she did so with no fanfare. She went back home to live with her parents. It was a good thing they had no children together, which really simplified things. She had not been surprised and she was thankful Reggie gave her ample time to move out of the house. She was not really going to stay in the Vegas area for long, anyway.

With the days dwindling down to Christmas vacation, Sara's class was busy preparing for their receptive and expressive final exam. She decided to honor Reggie's wishes by using his multiple-choice test using Scantron forms and she carried this over to all of the classes that he was supposed to be teaching in the fall semester. It was only fair, as the reaction papers, labs, book review, and class notes were on this test.

She decided to follow her own receptive test for the second half of the exam. Reggie had no issues with that and he was happy she would continue with the written portion which he had used every semester in 101. It would show who actually had read the workbook and Drolsbaugh/Kane books.

"Sara . . ." Should he tell her about the NDE he had in the hospital? Yes, absolutely. He believed in full transparency with her. "I had an experience in the hospital that you should be aware of. Can you sit back and just listen without interrupting? Please reserve judgment until I am done."

He was very nervous about telling her all this information, but it would be a good measuring stick to see how much she supported him and believed in him. So, he went ahead and told her the whole story. As he was explaining what happened, his eyes stayed on her face to gauge her reaction. Like he predicted, it ranged from surprise to shock. But she did not interrupt him even once. When he was finished, he was exhausted.

"Please do not ever talk about this with anyone except me. Promise? I plan to tell Dad later what happened, but without Mom there." Sara nodded solemnly and he smiled back at her. "Do you believe anything I just said to you?"

Sara signed YES YES YES BELIEVE YOU ME. She mouthed as she signed so he understood what she was telling him. Their hands were still clasped together as they talked for a while. They huddled to exchange ideas about her classes and arrange a group trip to DeafWorld Expo for their students during Christmas break. It was an exciting time for them and the first time most of the LVCC students would get to be a part of the deaf community. There were many logistics involved, but she would go talk to Dean Roya about the expenses and get permission to go ahead with the trip.

Final exams were uneventful. The grades were predictable in that students who were serious did well and those who were unprepared found themselves with lower grades on their transcripts. LVCC became a ghost town by December 23rd and professors submitted their grades on the Banner system. Everyone handed in signed hard copy roster grade sheets to their departments and parties started all over campus. The foreign language department was no exception.

By this time, Reggie was making great progress with his ASL. Using the online resources after class in the lab was greatly helping him. Plus, he worked with many students both one-on-one and in groups preparing for their exams so by this point, he had all of the signs and phrases down pat. It amazed Sara how much he learned in such a short time. It is true that a deaf person learns ASL very quickly, much faster than a hearing person. This was born from necessity, as deaf people relied on their eyes and not their ears to communicate with others.

Chapter 21

Something did happen as Christmas drew closer. Only one week remained before December 25th. Reggie would never forget the day. Sara and he were at Grand Canal Shoppes, enjoying a ride on a gondola on the water. They had opted for an indoor ride rather than outside, as it looked like it might rain sometime soon. They had gotten lucky, arriving just before the long lines started for the popular gondola rides. People didn't have to fly all the way to Italy anymore for this kind of experience. It was almost like the real thing.

This shopping center was one of the most popular tourist attractions on the Strip. Back in 1999, Sheldon Adelson announced his plans to build a pseudo-Venice. There had been a lot of skepticism from people including Reggie's father who had laughed it off. To everyone's surprise, the Venetian Resort-Hotel-Casino was a resounding success. Adelson flew in Sophia Loren from Italy to ride the first gondola boat. She wore a smashing red suit and she looked positively ageless, the envy of billions of women all over the world. She remarked to reporters that she could barely tell the difference between the Venetian and her native Venice! That sealed the deal and just like in "Field of Dreams", the tourists came in droves.

Gondolas like the one they were on glided through waterways through the resort's unique shopping center with over 4,000 fancy suites. The Venetian would go on to win the prize of being the world's largest AAA Five Diamond resort. Its sister property, the Palazzo, would also be bestowed this distinguished honor. Both hotels were associated with the Sands Convention Center. Max Kelleher had the opportunity to get in on the ground floor as part of the Family business, but he had declined and he never could live it down.

When Sara and Reggie were enjoying the atmosphere and laughing at the Santas walking around the mall, they could see two mannequins who were really people that did not move. Their favorite part of the shopping experience there was to watch people react when the mannequins made a sudden move and scared people out of their wits. It was kind of mean, but always fun to watch. Once, Reggie had watched them do that all day when he was younger.

Once the gondola trip was done, they got off the boat and deliberated what to do next. It was a whirlwind day of window shopping. They both were not the compulsive buyer types. That was another thing he really liked about Sara. Reggie knew people who thought nothing of buying $500 worth of clothes in one afternoon, even a $200 pair of jeans! Another friend hid her credit card bills from her spouse and he figured this was financial infidelity if you wanted to call it that.

When the day drew to a close, the connection he had with Sara became deeper and stronger. They both knew that day had been a special one, the first of many to come. His prediction proved to be prophetic. Vacation days went by very quickly. They spent a lot of time together, sightseeing the Strip.

As Reggie had grown up there, he showed Sara the insider's tour because he knew the area like the back of his hand. They went to all of the major hotels, touching upon them for a little while for Sara to get a taste of them. He was curious which one she liked the best. They saw CityCenter (ARIA), Vdara, Mandarin Oriental, Palazzo, Caesar's Palace, Mandalay Bay, Luxor, Excalibur, MGM, Mirage, New York New York, Paris, Treasure Island, Palms, Rio, Flamingo, Harrah's, Monte Carlo, Planet Hollywood, and Circus Circus.

Their favorite stop was the Stratosphere. Reggie told Sara it opened in 1996 and it was the most unique ride in all of Vegas. He could see, though, that something new was being built across the Strip from the Luxor. Some kind of new ride. Nobody really knew what it was just yet, but there was no doubt it would be really amazing. That empty spot was where NBC had filmed the TV show "America Ninja Warrior" so it would be filled with the new attraction. NBC had not been happy when they heard of the construction project. But there was nothing they could do about it.

Finally, after a couple of weeks, they were all done with the hotels. They sat in Reggie's folks' living room, lazily wasting a few hours before dinner. It was Sunday night and the DeafWorld Expo was slated to open early the next morning at the Luxor Hotel. That had been because of his father's connections. Winter in Vegas was normally very expensive, but Max had finagled a great deal for this event's organizers and the hotels were all booked with thousands of deaf and hearing attendees who were arriving every hour. The four of them had contemplated going to the Luxor Sunday night, but it would have been too much for them.

Instead, Reggie and Sara booked a hotel room for Monday early morning through Thursday afternoon. The expo was scheduled to last two days and they wanted more time to see other sights in

Vegas that Sara had never seen before. She also wanted to return to a few of the hotels and maybe gamble some money for the fun of it.

"Whoo, Sara! Have you ever seen so much in just two weeks? I bet not!" Reggie laughed and made himself comfortable on the leather couch. Sara looked too tired to even open her eyes. It was funny that she did not have to look at him as if he had been signing to her. He still could not remember most of his ASL, but he was slowly getting there.

Sara opened her right eye and stuck her tongue out. "Never in my life! But I loved it. Especially the human mannequins. I would love to go back and just watch for a few hours. Would that be OK? We could eat the gelato and have popcorn like it was a movie or play!"

He liked that idea and signed YES GOOD IDEA! Now only if he could do that with any ASL phrase. He couldn't wait for that day to come. Sara had packed a bag for several days so they were all set. They went to sleep very quickly, exhausted from all of the hotel hopping. It seemed like only a few seconds when the vibrating alarm went off under his pillow. Reggie groaned and took out the clock. It read 6:00 a.m.

Sara had teased him before they went to bed that every time he woke up, it was like a California earthquake. She felt bad for him because hearing people's alarms had melodious music playing, birds singing, anything that sounded pleasant. So, when he woke up Monday morning, he looked over at Sara who was trying to catch a few more winks. After a couple of minutes, she rolled over to face him and opened her eyes with a sigh. He laughed and gave her a kiss on the lips.

"Impossible to sleep through that earthshaking alarm of yours! Oh well. A small sacrifice to make to be with you, honey." Sara giggled and reached out for him, but he teasingly stayed just out of range. He wagged his index finger at her.

"Naughty girlfriend, you are! Just for that, I am going into the shower now. We have a long day ahead of us at Luxor. See you in a few minutes unless you want to be my shower partner!" He walked backwards, feeling the wall, keeping his eyes on Sara who looked beautiful in bed. Heck, she looked fabulous anywhere, anytime. What was he talking about? She was just gorgeous. No matter what she was wearing! Once he reached the bathroom door, he turned around and flicked the light on. The shower was uneventful and he got dressed very quickly. Sara did the same and they were out of the house in half an hour.

"I am very nervous, Sara . . ." Reggie was in the passenger seat while Sara was driving. One of his quirks was that he preferred the hearing person to drive especially now that he had to lipread instead of watch the signs. It was very difficult to keep his eyes on the road and focus on the other person talking. They passed street after street and before long, they could see the Luxor right near the airport.

My God, there were so many deaf people walking into the hotel between the huge lions out front. Reggie felt all flushed in his face. As their car pulled up to the front, a valet ran over to open Sara's door and gave her a ticket. Reggie slowly opened his door, stepped out, and stretched to his full height. A porter came over and asked them if they needed help with their bags. Reggie had figured he would ask them that, as he had stayed at many hotels on the Strip before and that was always the first question asked.

Sara had been watching and she smiled. It was like Reggie was a hearing person for a minute or two, not even having to lipread someone to know what was said. It was something he had taught in ASL 101. Only thirty percent of what is uttered is visible on the lips. That meant deaf people had to guess the other seventy percent by guesswork and contextual clues. She pulled the lever inside the car, on the driver's side, and the trunk opened. Reggie walked over and took out their bags. Then, he closed the door and gave the valet a thumbs up, forking over a couple dollars' tip.

They walked inside and Reggie could see the huge Sphinx right in front of him. So many memories as he glanced around the lobby. There was T&T's upstairs, right near the escalator. Luckily, not many people were arriving at this early hour so they made fast work of their sign-in. The people at the counter recognized Reggie and they all smiled in his direction. A few saw Sara and their eyebrows shot up. This was new! He had never brought a woman to the Luxor before.

It was almost 9:00 on the dot when Reggie and Sara came back down to the first floor. Reggie knew where the convention was and many people would lose their way, as the ballrooms were in a different building behind the main one. Not many knew that and he motioned for Sara to follow him. They passed some slot machines, the jewelry store where Max had worked, a Starbucks, more slot machines, and then they walked down a long hallway. Reggie looked at Sara, holding her hand. She looked so confused, poor thing! But Reggie knew the place very well and confidently strode on. Her expression was like, "Are you sure we are in the right direction?" He nodded to her, answering telepathically.

Finally, they had arrived around the corner and there were many people waiting at the doors already. The spa and salon were on the opposite side of the waiting area. Reggie had never gotten to try that place yet and wanted Sara to go with him there once the expo ended. He already had made an appointment for Wednesday. It was something to look forward to—a manicure, pedicure, the works!

Sara was obviously overwhelmed by the huge number of signers already waiting for the big doors to open. They were pre-registered. The organizers had been very smart to encourage registrants to print out tickets so there would be much shorter lines for entrance. Right on the dot, at 9 a.m., the doors opened. Reggie looked at Sara and laughed, shrugging his shoulders. She looked back at him with a quizzical look on her face.

"Don't you get it? For once, there is no DST . . . D-S-T . . . Deaf Standard Time!"

Sara stared at him for a few seconds and slowly her face lit up in comprehension. No wonder she had been confused. Even though she taught ASL and knew about DST, it still had not registered with her immediately. For Reggie, he had been around deaf people for many years, being deaf himself, so it was second nature for him to notice whether things started on time at a deaf event or not. Most of the time, these things did not and he was used to it. It never fazed him when a deaf event started late. That was just how it worked in "Eyeth", a moniker he had seen for the Deaf world.

"Sara . . ." Reggie waited for her to turn in his direction even as everyone else pushed and shoved trying to gain entrance into the huge conference room for the expo. "This is just how it works in Eyeth . . ." He was echoing his thoughts as they ran through his mind. Strangely, he could remember all this info, but not the ASL itself!

"Eyeth? What the heck is that? I never heard of that."

"Yeah, think about it. E-A-R for hearing people who process information by hearing, right? How do deaf people process information coming to them? With their eyes, right? So, E-Y-E and then add T-H!" HE finished with a flourish and grinned at her in triumph, as it was just brilliant of someone to even think of that humorous side of the deaf world.

Sara laughed and slapped Reggie on his right shoulder. "That is so silly, but funny! I like it a lot. Let's go see what Eyeth has to offer here!" She put her left hand inside his right hand and tugged gently, motioning her head towards the doors. Reggie was really nervous because of his lack of ASL skills. He had no idea how people would react to him voicing without any signs. Nobody knew what had happened over the past few months with his accident and subsequent recovery. He just hoped it all went very smoothly and people did not pity him once Sara explained it to them.

Sure enough, they spent the whole first day telling people through her what did happen to him. Once they knew the story, they were very understanding and compassionate to Reggie. He even recognized some faces from past deaf events and it was funny because Sara had never gone to deaf events before, even though she was an ASL professor. Everyone was surprised to see him as word had gotten around about the hit and run on the news.

The expo was a great experience for both of them. Reggie was still struggling with ASL, but with each passing day he was closer to fluency. But it would be quite some time before that happened. There were many vendors at the convention center for them to look at. Sara and Reggie walked past all of the tables and watched the shows that were featured all day. Before they knew it, 5 p.m. came and went. They had to leave and decided to grab dinner inside the mall between the Luxor and Mandalay Bay. Reggie wanted to sample that hamburger place, as he could remember the juicy, delicious burgers he'd enjoyed with his dad when walking through between the Luxor and Mandalay Bay.

Chapter 22

Marcus Brossler was absolutely furious and insulted. He spent the whole day walking around the Luxor Hotel trying to figure out where Sara and Reggie were. He had been hanging around the lobby with a book in his hand and he even had a hat on to disguise himself somewhat. If either Reggie or Sara had seen him, he would have been in a load of trouble, as he knew that Sara had taken out an order of protection on him recently. He was not sure if Sara had told Reggie about that yet, but he was taking no chances.

Marcus had a huge body frame for someone who was average height. He had spent many hours in the gym working out for the time when he would confront Sara and fight any man that came between him and her. He vowed to crush Reggie's skull once and for all. Too bad Reggie survived that accident. If only! But that would happen soon enough if he had anything to say about it.

Their relationship had started off with a lot of promise. They had met in a bar. He knew all of the clichés about bars and it had been a private joke between them. They were the only couple he knew that actually met in such a place. Ironically enough, the bar was on the Strip. He could not remember the name right now, but it was not far from the Luxor Hotel. He knew that Reggie's father was very influential in Strip real estate so he was being cautious about getting caught. There would seriously be hell to pay if everything did not go perfectly today with his plan of revenge. All he needed was the right time and place to strike.

He had breakfast on the second floor of the Luxor near the McDonald's. The food was always delicious. He loved the Big Breakfast which featured scrambled eggs, biscuit, sausage, bacon, and coffee. It filled him up and he did not know if there would be any time for lunch or dinner, as he would be following them the whole day to figure out when to intervene in their lives for the last time. Either way, he was going to make his presence known.

Would he succeed in getting rid of Reggie? He did not want to be overconfident. How dare Reggie snatch her from his life? Didn't all those years count for something? Just because his daddy was rich and famous did not mean he could just win Sara's heart and make him sloppy seconds. No sirree. That just would not wash. He had to be number one. He deserved it after all that time with Sara. Plus, he knew all about Reggie's reputation at LVCC as a professor with a bad attitude towards students. How could a guy like that win Sara's heart? He had to rescue her from Reggie's wiles!

Marcus spent the entire day looking for Reggie and Sara and had no luck. He was unable to enter the DeafWorld Expo because he was not registered for it. He had to make himself inconspicuous until the expo closed at 5 p.m. His patience was rewarded when he sat at an one-armed bandit (also known as a slot machine) just at the far edge of the Luxor's lobby near the Starbucks. With his hat and fake glasses, he was virtually unrecognizable. As he slowly put his quarter in the slot to try his luck for the thousandth time that afternoon, he saw them walk past him.

His body felt a sudden shot of adrenaline! He was ready for the perfect moment. Getting up, his butt felt sore from sitting on the stool for such a long time without a break. He kept his distance, knowing it only took one backward glance from either one to be caught and thrown in jail for a long time. He was skilled at these surveillance games, as he had studied criminal justice in college. Plus, those video games had taught him a thing or two.

Sara and Reggie walked up the stairs to the second floor and turned left. Obviously, they were headed to the mall next to the Luxor. That was just fine with him. There were many places to hide and blend into the crowds. Luckily, they had not gone outside the hotel. It was dinner time so perhaps that's what their plans were now. He walked past all of the stores and then saw them stop at one of the small restaurants on the right side. It was the hamburger joint! He had eaten there before. The food was really good. Interesting that they had picked that one.

Now he had to decide what to do. Stay behind and hope they did not take too long or just walk in and finish the job, hoping all of the customers were too shocked to do anything before he fled the scene? This was like admiring a chocolate cake. All of the anticipation was so much fun and it would make the taste even sweeter once he committed the dastardly deed. His hand reached into his pocket to touch the nine millimeter pistol. Of course, it was loaded, but the safety was off so it would not accidentally discharge. He was a crack shot and had practiced with it at the local shooting range. He even had taken the precaution of taking a refresher class on pistol safety just to be sure.

Seeing them enter the restaurant, he made a decision. One that would have ripple effects on everything that happened after that. Swallowing hard, he pushed all of his nervousness aside and girded himself up for the culmination of all the hard work and suffering that he had endured because of Reggie. This guy was really pissing him off, acting like he had even the remotest idea of what it took to be with Sara while he was left out in the cold. Not for long!

He pulled his shirt out and with his back to people walking past him, he took the pistol out of his front right pocket. He nestled it in his waist and threw the shirt over it. Time was approaching for him to do what he had set out to do. Turning around, he looked down at his pants and could not see the pistol stick out. Perfect. He forced himself to stay calm and took measured steps to the burger restaurant.

As he approached the entrance, a hostess stepped out of her spot behind the podium and smiled radiantly at him. "Do you want a table, sir? We are not crowded right now and the food is really delicious here!"

She was very pretty, petite, and had those big blue eyes that he had always liked in a woman. But today was not the time for him to admire a gorgeous woman. He had one goal in his mind.

"I have two friends in here that I would like to join. One is my girlfriend, Sara, and the other is a mutual friend, Reggie." That was smart, he realized. In some way, Reggie was a mutual person in their lives and there would be no threat seen now that he identified who Sara and Reggie were.

He was proven right when the hostess, whose name was Lisa as he saw her name badge for the first time, stepped back and put her right hand out to let him enter. Mission accomplished! He had not even thought of how to talk to someone so he could get inside, but he had done it. Mentally, he patted himself on the back and the rest was going to be clear sailing. His eyes roved across the dining area. This was going to be a little difficult. Many of the tables were booths and the ones in the back were hidden by very tall backstops made of wood. He had forgotten about that. No matter. That was not going to stop him now.

He looked back at Lisa and smiled, nodding. That way, he made sure to reassure her and his head turned to the front. Walking slowly, he turned his head right and left. This was kind of cool, like the Terminator did when he hunted for Sarah O'Connor when he came back from the future to assassinate her. That was one of his favorite movies.

Ah, he had found them! They were seated in the corner way in the back. No wonder he had not seen them when he entered. Moistening his lips, he felt like the hunter about to go for the kill. Just a few steps to go. He saw Sara turn to him and her eyes became as big as saucers. She was definitely shocked to see him there. Good! He wanted to put the fear of God in her and have her watch as he snuffed Reggie's life. Then, she would never leave him again.

Sara had been enjoying her meal with Reggie like never before. They were comfortably seated with privacy, away from everyone else. Even though Reggie normally wanted to sit with a view of the whole restaurant, this time he had decided against it. He just wanted to look at her! She thought that was so romantic and it was fortunate that she had seen Marcus approaching first. This was totally unexpected and she could feel the fear spreading throughout her body.

She could hear Reggie's voice. "Sara, you look like you have seen a ghost! What is wrong? Are you OK?"

She shook her head and mouthed, "Do not even move. My ex-boyfriend is standing a few feet away from us! Oh my God, he has a gun in his hand!" She was paralyzed and there was no escape for them. Then, all of a sudden, out of the corner of her right eye, she saw a blur. Someone tackled Marcus from behind! What was this? The pistol clattered on the floor as Marcus lost his grip on it. She pounced from her seat and dived for the gun so he could not grab it again.

Marcus could not believe it. Just a few seconds away from victory! Someone rammed into him as he was lifting the pistol to aim at the couple that he hated. His head hit the floor hard and he could feel his nose smash into the tile. Blood gushed from his face and became a puddle. His eyes flooded with the blood that was quickly becoming bigger. Where was that damn gun? Rage flooded his muscles and he strained to push this other guy off him, but it was futile. He realized that he had been overpowered and outmuscled. Surprise had been the deciding factor.

Resigned, he relaxed his body and lay there waiting for the police to come. Damn it, so close! But he was proud that he had attempted to end their relationship. His eyes could see two pairs of shoes under the table where Sara and Reggie were seated. Just a few feet away! Suddenly, he was turned over so his back was mired in the ever-growing pool of blood on the floor. He faced the ceiling and got his first look at the man who had thrown a wrench in his plans.

Now he understood why the other guy had been successful. He was huge. Not just huge. Enormous! Even his own body paled beside this guy's. He looked like a Green Beret or Navy SEAL. He had a crew cut and a chiseled face with a prominent jawline covered with black stubble. Two piercing green eyes stared at him and he knew right then that this was no ordinary mortal. Probably was ex-military. Why was someone like that willing to risk his life and how did he even know what was about to transpire?

It was training, pure and simple. Anticipation, preparation, reaction. That was drilled into elite military soldiers and he had just witnessed it in action now. Just his rotten luck that this guy had been here. Or was he there on purpose, following him? Did Reggie have a bodyguard because of his father? His brain rattled with the possibilities. In any case, he was cooked and definitely off to prison for what he had tried to do. His hopes were extinguished. No Mexico for him, not for a very long time. Sighing, he closed his eyes and shut out the world.

Chapter 23

Reggie could not believe what he was witnessing. After Sara looked at him with such a frightened look on her face and her eyes wide open like he had never seen them before, he just had to turn to his left and see what was going on. his brain exploded as he saw this short, stocky guy sprawled out on the floor in a puddle of blood, his eyes closed and arms spread out. Another guy had his knee on his chest, glaring down at his face. He looked like someone you would never want to mess around with.

Reggie wondered if Sara was in trouble with one of those guys. Actually, if the second guy wanted to kill them, he already would have. Then, Reggie realized Sara was not sitting across from him anymore. Where was she? Feeling a lot of anxiety, Reggie started to panic. his eyes searched for her and he saw her on the other side of the room grasping the pistol, aimed at the guy on the floor. A pistol? Someone had tried to kill them!

First, a hit and run. Now, a botched killing. Reggie wondered why he was such a target all of a sudden. Knowing his dad's involvement in the Family, there had to be a connection. his heart beat so fast and he was afraid he would hyperventilate. What was going on? He felt like he had to contact his dad immediately to get to the bottom of this.

Chapter 24

Dirk Ramses prided himself on another job well done. He had been a Navy SEAL after finishing his first tour in the Marine Corps. He was now a private contractor working for Salvatore Ballardi and he had been hired just yesterday to follow Reggie Kelleher around 24/7 for a few days. He was supposed to take turns with a friend who also was a Navy SEAL in the same Team Three that he had been in. They trusted each other implicitly.

He had first thought this was a silly assignment and he spent the whole day inside the expo shadowing them without seeming too obvious. Luckily, he knew ASL to some extent so he blended into the DeafWorld Expo quite easily and nobody became suspicious about his presence. There had been no incidents inside the convention center and now here he was, thwarting an actual shooting. The guy on the floor looked familiar. Was that the ex-boyfriend? Yes, it was! He had reviewed hundreds of photographs supplied by Ballardi before starting this job so he could be prepared for whoever he ran into. That was part of his work ethic. He could still remember the other day when Sal called him in to assign him this job.

"Ram, I have a job for you! Right up your alley." Sal the Pal sat behind his mahogany desk, sitting in a lush, black leather chair. His arms rested on the sides.

"I owe someone a favor and promised him a nice surprise so this is it. Do you know who Maxwell Kelleher is?"

Ram was his nickname, as people thought his last name was too strange, reminding them of the Egyptian despot who had lost everything to Moses. He also did not like the name Dirk as it sounded like a particular piece of his anatomy that he never wanted to hear as referring to him. It was like that word 'wenus' which was actually the skin off the elbow—people always thought it was a part of the penis for some reason.

Maxwell Kelleher? "Of course, I know who that is. The real estate mogul guy you used to work with years ago. What about him?" His curiosity was piqued. What did this have to do with anything?

"Ram, listen carefully. Max Kelleher has a son named Reggie and there might be someone going after him. He was almost killed in a hit and run a while ago and I am afraid for his safety. Can you and a partner take turns watching him for a week or so? It would allay my nerves and I would feel better doing this."

He had been given a pile of pictures with names and job titles to review. Then, he started the job soon after. Now he was sure that Sal would be very happy to be proven right. Time to call Sal and let him know the job was done. Even better for him, as he was paid a lot of money even if the job was cut short.

He whipped out his cell phone and speed-dialed Sal. This phone was one of those disposables so it could not be traced by anyone. Once he used it and the job was done, he could just throw it away and never be bothered with that phone again. All transactions were done on a cash-only basis. He kept his eye on Marcus who was still lying on the floor, unmoving.

"Sal? Guess what. Yes, the job is done. I will send you a photo. Sara and Reggie are fine. She was with him at a burger joint and

Marcus tried to aim his pistol, but I tackled him in time. Sara has the gun now pointed at him. All is good. Please wire the remainder of the money. Thanks. You take care too."

Ram closed the disposable cell phone and put it in his right front pocket. Time to focus on the matter at hand before the cops arrived. His left hand grasped a business card that he had just taken out of another pocket. He better vamoose before any more trouble started.

"Here's my card, Reggie. Just hold onto it and call that number today if you can. I really gotta go, but just know I am one of the good guys and just saved your life. Hope you appreciate that!" Ram's mouth curled into a slight smile and he saluted Reggie. "I am never going to see you again nor will you see me. Just remember the name Sal Ballardi."

In a few seconds, Ram was gone as if he had never been there. He had put on a hat so people would see less of his face and not have so much description for the police to follow up on.

Reggie held the business card in his hand. It was quite a simple, ordinary looking card, no different than the hundreds he'd seen in his lifetime, except for the fact that there was only one line printed with no name, nothing else: 847-555-5555 CALL ASAP. What was this? Why would anyone want to give out a card like that? This whole thing just became curiouser and curiouser. Reggie's forehead wrinkled as he was deep in thought. He hastily put the card away and it was just as well because two cops arrived at the restaurant with guns out, their eyes roaming the dining room in anticipation.

One cop, Officer Redding, saw Sara with the gun and motioned for her to put it on the floor very slowly. She complied quickly, knowing any delay would endanger her life. The other cop, Officer Beck, walked over to the guy on the floor and pointed the gun at him.

"Who are you and what happened here?" The cop was in no mood for any funny business today. He had had a bad day already with many incidents. His jaw was sore from someone else's punch during an altercation when resisting arrest. But he had decided to continue on his shift instead of going to the hospital. Now he was starting to regret that decision, as he had every right to be medically treated.

Sara yelled, "My boyfriend sitting back there is deaf so you need to speak slowly for him. The guy on the floor is my ex, Marcus Brossler, who stalked us and just tried to kill us. Someone tackled him from behind and the gun jumped from his hand to the floor. I ran over and grabbed the gun to point at him and prevent him from doing anything else. Then, this stranger ran away, leaving us. You just missed him by minutes." She was breathing heavily when she finished.

The cop near her who had taken her gun nodded and whipped out his notepad. "Your name, please. I need it for my notes."

"My name is Sara Zaslow. Let me spell it for you—Z-A-S-L-O-W. My ex boyfriend is on the floor, Marcus Brossler. I am pretty sure he has a record. My date over there is Reggie Kelleher."

Redding did a double-take. Kelleher? "Any relation to the mogul?" Now that would really be something if the guy sitting there was his son or something.

Sara nodded. "His son. Remember the hit and run a few weeks ago? Same guy. Someone just tried to kill him, a different hitman than the driver then. Now do you believe me?" She sincerely hoped these were smart cops so they would not arrest her, as she was totally innocent.

"I gotta call this in. Way over my pay grade. Please remain on scene, but you can go sit with Reggie if you want. I will hold onto the gun. Beck, put the handcuffs on Brossler for now so he won't get away." Beck called in the incident and made a quick job out of it.

"The lieu will be here pretty quickly and probably everyone else who is part of the top brass. Do you want me to call your father?" He looked at Sara who then mouthed what he said silently. Why was she doing that? Ah, for Reggie. That was one sharp lady thinking on her feet. Not many gals would have had the temerity to hold a gun on someone even if in self defense.

Redding pressed a button on his radio. "Dispatch, please call Maxwell Kelleher and tell him to get over here quickly! We are at Best Burgers in the mall at Luxor Hotel. His son and a friend were in danger, but now they are safe. Thanks!" Wow, amazing how luck changed on a dime! Here he was, first on the scene as ranking officer with an attempted homicide on the son of one of Vegas' most well-known citizens. He had heard of other cops being this lucky, but not him.

Chapter 25

Reggie continued to sit there, staring down at Marcus. After Sara explained who he was and why he was there, Reggie slowly pieced things together. It was probably not another attempted hit by a Family "employee" because Marcus was after both Sara and him out of jealousy. He feared for his safety and for Sara's. But then again, Rocks would be rotting in prison for a long time because of this and they were safe.

Footsteps drew closer and he felt the ground shake. Was that someone running towards him? Reggie's body tensed and he glanced over to Sara who also turned to face the person coming towards them. Was that Dad? Yes! Reggie must have registered surprise on his face, as Dad quickly came over to hug him tight. Dad said something in Reggie's ear, but he could not understand what Dad was saying. Reggie's eyes searched out for Sara sitting across the table and she interpreted, "I'm so sorry, son! Are you OK? I could never bear to lose you."

That was Dad, all right. He was always in touch with his feelings and made sure Reggie knew how much Dad loved him. He gently pushed Dad away and put both hands on Dad's cheeks. They were moist from his tears and he felt safe with Dad there.

"What is going on? Why is someone protecting me and Sara?"

"Son, I just found out the story. We better sit down for this. I am going to sign to Sara and she will mouth to you without voice so the cops won't be able to overhear anything. We better make it quick because I know the chief of detectives and other brass will be coming soon.

"Here goes . . ." He went on to explain about his meeting with Sal the Pal and his realization that the 'favor' promised to him had been 24/7 protection for some time. Ballardi had felt remorse for the hit and run. It was a stroke of luck for them because the protection had just started yesterday so they had been saved by an associate of the Family. Reggie's theory went out the window! He had had it all reversed, but he really did not care at the time. He numbly watched Sara continue to mouth what Dad was explaining, but he had already figured it out.

Would this nightmare ever end? First, Reggie had to start all over with his signing and he came close to dying twice! Second, he almost lost his job but Sara had saved his hide by intervening with Dean Esfahani to allow him to work in the lab until the following summer, when he should be back to normal again remembering the ASL he'd had before. Shaking his head, he thought how this all was like a soap opera. In fact, he had been addicted to "Days of Our Lives" (also referred to as DOOL) back in the mid-1990's with so many plot twists. This definitely qualified.

Suddenly, Sara was not mouthing anymore and she looked at Reggie with concern. He was suddenly feeling cold and could not think anymore. He felt woozy and weak, not being able to keep his eyes open. Why was he feeling this way? It was like he was not even present and suddenly all was black.

Chapter 26

What was wrong with Reggie? Sara saw him just slump onto the table with his face resting near the plate of half-eaten food. Max jumped up and yelled to the cops, "Call 911 now! My son passed out!" Reggie was not moving and Max was really worried. Never in his life had he been so scared other than the day he got that phone call about Reggie being hit by a car and taken to the ER. How had the guy known that the gunman was gunning for Reggie and Sara? His mind felt like marbles were bouncing all over inside and he could not think about what would happen five minutes from now. Hopefully, the ambulance would arrive soon.

He heard a cell phone ring and recognized the ringtone as his own. Who could be calling him at a time like this? Could it be Viv? She did not know about this incident yet. He was not planning to tell her for awhile. She took medicine for her heart and he did not want a heart attack to happen. Opening the phone, he put it next to his ear. What? It was Sal the Pal! He would know that voice anywhere. Why was Ballardi calling him at the same time this incident happened? His suspicions grew every second.

"Hello, Sal—what brings you to call me?" Max was in no mood for pleasantries especially if Sal was behind this attempted hit. The nerve of that guy to call as if to gloat about how easy it was to kill his only child.

"Max, is Reggie all right? My associate just left the crime scene and he's the one who saved him and Sara . . ."

Max could not believe his ears. Was Sal saying he was the one who had saved the couple from a certain death at the hand of Marcus Brossler? He wanted to listen some more.

The voice continued in its baritone. "Listen, remember the last time we met and I told you I would surprise you with a favor?" The phone became quiet. Max thought back to their meeting over the phone and realized what Sal was referring to. He recalled every word verbatim.

"Yes, I remember, Sal. You mean, you sent that ex-military guy to shadow my son for a few days just to see what would happen? That was very smart! I wish I had done the same thing. How can I ever repay you for this? You saved Reggie's life!" Max became overcome by emotion and was unable to continue any further. He started to choke up and cry.

Sal could hear Max's tears over the phone and understood. "It's OK. I was really mortified when Rocks went after your son. Know that I did not condone what he did, nor would I ever send anyone after your family. It was my fault for not keeping him on a tighter leash. So, the least I could do was to protect your son from any more violence against him and it looks like I was right on the money!"

Max wiped his tears with a handkerchief and nodded to himself. He was beyond relieved that Sal had looked after him without being asked. Now he was sure that everything was fine between him and the Family.

"So, all is copacetic? I have nothing to worry about with my son and wife, plus myself? All is square?"

"Yes, Max. The past is past. Let's let bygones be bygones." Sal was satisfied that Max had done what he did in good faith. Max was a good man, very professional, and would not do anything to hurt the Family. Time to just leave him alone.

"Also, I will alert all of the other Families to never bother you again, Max. You have my word on that. Can I tell them what happened to Reggie and Sara?"

Max thought about it for a second and whispered in a low voice, "Yes, it is fine for you to do that. I am sorry that I cannot talk any more right now. I just don't know what to say. Thank you for your friendship. It means a lot to me." He hung up his cell phone and his attention turned back to Sara.

"Thank you also for being with Reggie and protecting him the best you can. You already knew this, but I wanted to tell you officially that you have my utmost blessing to be with him. I think you will . . . actually, I know . . . you will . . . make a great daughter-in-law. Vivian and I want to welcome you to our ranks. It is interesting that everyone signs fluently, three hearing people and Reggie."

Max could not help but smile wanly as he finished what he said. Sara, even in the midst of all of this commotion, silently nodded. Then their moment was interrupted by two EMT's who had just arrived at the scene. They got busy, putting Reggie on the table, checking his vitals.

One of the EMT's immediately got on his radio to alert the ER of their imminent arrival, as it appeared to be life-threatening. They opened up a stretcher and gently put Reggie on it. Reggie was still out of it, as they hurried back to the ambulance. Sara followed them as they ran as fast as they could. Reggie was hooked up to a respirator and an IV for body fluids to get him hydrated. As their figures disappeared around the corner, Max buried his face in his hands and cried again. What was the world coming to, anyway?

Chapter 27

It was pandemonium at the same hospital where Reggie had spent weeks in the ICU. The EMT's brought him in and Dr. Shapiro happened to be on duty that day. When he got the call about Reggie Kelleher, he did a double-take and could not believe that another attempt had been made on this young man. Yet, nothing had actually happened to him physically. It was probably a culmination of emotional, mental, and physical stress stemming from the recovery after the hit and run accident. Reggie would be OK.

He got on the computer and reviewed the notes from the ambulance EMT's. All of the information fit the profile for PTSD, post-traumatic stress disorder. Reggie's body had collapsed from everything and the last straw had been the attempted shooting that just book place in the restaurant where the EMT's found him. He had to reassure Reggie's parents and tell them this was nothing to worry about. He knew this whole thing was scary to witness and it looked a lot worse than it actually was.

Sure enough, there was Max and Vivian Kelleher coming towards him as he sat at the computer near Reggie's room. He stood up and took a few steps towards them. "There is nothing to worry about . . ." He explained about PTSD for a few minutes and reassured them that Reggie would be fine. His body was just in shock and this was not life-threatening. He could see Max's body posture sag as he explained the situation.

"I have seen this with veterans coming back home from the Middle East also. This will be very cathartic for Reggie. His body needs absolute bed rest and we will be monitoring him very carefully. Feel free to go into his room, but please do not touch him. It is best to leave him be. You can just watch him and keep an eye on him if you wish. But there's really nothing more you can do right now."

Max and Vivian both felt immense relief. Vivian loved her son absolutely and without any limitation. She could remember back when Reggie was only eight months old and they found out he was deaf. She and her husband had worked tirelessly, attending ASL classes near them at the local school for the deaf, going to deaf events, networking with other parents who had deaf children, and much more. Interestingly, most of those parents gave up on becoming fluent in ASL and this had bothered Max and Viv a lot. They never gave up and finally they were pretty close to fluent by the time Reggie was in fifth grade.

She smiled at the memories of their dinner conversations every day. Since Reggie was an only child, he had their full attention. Max had insisted on discussing current events with their son like the Kennedys did on a daily basis. As a result, Reggie was very aware of what was going on in the world. He even had been the #1 trivia guy in high school and nobody was able to stump him with a question. He had a photographic memory for many things although it was nothing like Marilu Henner who had the uncanny ability to remember events from every single day of her life such as what she was wearing, what she ate, where she was, etc. Only eight people in the entire world had that kind of memory.

This was probably why Reggie was picking up ASL so quickly even though he had to start all over from scratch. Already, in less than a month, he was able to converse at their dinner table. It was a refreshing 180 degree turn, as the hearing parents were now teaching their deaf son conversational ASL. All three of them were enjoying this a great deal, as Reggie learned how much patience was required to learn ASL at the fluency level. He began to understand the needs of his own college students much more

Chapter 28

Reggie lay in the hospital bed, unmoving. But he was lingering near the ceiling and looking down at himself. Not again! This was the second time he had left his body and he could hear Mom's thoughts as she looked back on his childhood. Yes, it had been really cool to trade places with his parents, becoming the student learning ASL. He also could feel her pain in remembering the travails on the road to ASL fluency along with his dad's who had a harder time learning than Mom. Why was it that women had a much easier time than men? Was it because they were more sensitive? The same could go for the "helping professions" such as social work, education, psychology, nursing, and others.

Feeling a pull upwards, he did not resist. The last time this happened, he had tried to stick around, but it had been too sudden for him to realize what was going on. This time, Reggie was more prepared. The same tunnel sides whooshed past him and he felt the warmth and love surrounding him again. Was this the second and last time he would go through this NDE? Would he be able to come back and live his life with Sara?

In an instant, he found himself standing on top of a cliff overlooking the most beautiful valley he'd ever laid his eyes on. The colors were bright and vivid. He tried to remember the name of the movie with Robin Williams and Cuba Gooding, Jr., the one with the husband looking for his wife in the netherworld after her suicide. It did not matter now. Wait, yes! It was "What Dreams May Come." Then, he realized he would be seeing his relatives again! Sure enough, he could see figures approaching. There was Arielle! She came running and gave him this loving hug. She had grown a little bit since he saw her before. Her blonde hair shone even brighter and she was so beautiful. All four of his grandparents stood near her, looking at him with obvious pride on their faces.

"We are so happy you are OK. Don't worry, you will be going back again. We just wanted to see you and ease your worries! It is a miracle that you are here again and we could not afford to miss this opportunity. We also wanted to let you know that when you go back, you will have a new gift similar to what Stella Frabizi has. Remember that show you went to with Deanna?"

He stood there, open-mouthed. Are you kidding me? He was going to be a medium, communicating with those on the Other Side? Instantly, he thought of James van Praagh, Dannion Brinkley, John Edward, Lisa Williams, Theresa Caputo, John Holland, and others who he had admired on TV. He was going to join that elite club! But how was this possible? He had to find out!

He could remember everything about the life review as it rolled out before him again. The same negative incidents showed themselves first, but it was much shorter than before. Then the review showed him as he had been after the accident, a very changed man with a kinder approach to life, treating others with the respect that they deserved, spending time with Sara and his parents. His temper tantrums were nonexistent. Then he got the surprise of his life. He saw students talking to each other out in the hallway and the number one topic was about him, how much nicer he had been after he returned, their appreciation of his sense of humor and patience. He watched as they prepared the banner and how they were smiling as they worked on it together in the classroom early that morning before he entered.

Looking at Arielle and his grandparents, his thoughts were transmitted to them. They all nodded and he got the feeling they approved of who he had become lately on earth. Now it was his time to return again and unlike last time, he had no qualms doing so. He had a huge job to do and he was ready to move on with his life as a professor and a medium. Of course, he would be disbelieved and mocked, but he also had the opportunity to give comfort and peace to many people. He vowed not to charge exorbitant amounts of money so that anyone could get to appreciate his gift.

His body felt heavy all over and he opened his eyes, seeing the ceiling lights of his hospital room. He was back! It seemed like a ton of bricks was resting on every part of his body. That was how tired he felt. It took quite some effort to turn his head sideways. He could see his parents and Sara sitting near each other, reading and talking. In his peripheral vision, he could see several figures on the opposite side of the room. Slowly, he turned his head to the left just to make sure he was seeing things correctly. Yes, they were still there, but he did not recognize them at all.

"Hi guys! I am back. You can't keep a good man down!" Reggie chuckled and then groaned at the pain he felt all over his body. He really did need this bedrest. "How long have I been here?"

Commotion ensued as his parents and Sara rushed over to his right side. Sara grasped his hand and her eyes were filling up with tears. His folks stood there looking at him tenderly.

"Honey . . ." Sara was obviously trying to compose herself and she was signing. "We are so happy to see you awake. Two days! We have been here the whole time."

Wait! Reggie understood every single word she signed! But, ironically, he could not move his arms due to the enormous fatigue he felt. "Sara, this might sound like it's out of left field, but did your parents pass on within a few months of each other? I sense that your mother was first then your father? And you have a lot of anger towards him for not being a good husband and father when you were growing up."

Sara flinched and looked around. "How did you know this? I never told you anything like that." She looked very uncomfortable and she was backing away from him.

He really did have the gift! It was just natural for him to see the spirits standing there and communicate what they were thinking.

"Yes, they are standing right across the room from you. Your dad is very apologetic and really feels remorse for everything he did to your mom and you. He has this sorrowful look on his face. I get a 'J' name—John, Josh? I am leaning more towards John even though that is such a common name."

"John, yes! I never even mentioned him to you, ever. Not in all those hours together in the office and sightseeing in Vegas recently. Is he really here?"

Reggie sighed and nodded. "Your mom is standing next to him. She is radiant and is excited to be able to communicate with you. What is it with butterflies? Have you been seeing them at home?"

Sara gasped and signed YES EVERY-MORNING BUTTERFLIES HOUSE ALL-OVER and then she voiced it, maybe to emphasize that what he had just said was true. Sara was shocked and thoughts were flooding her mind. What had happened to Reggie since he fainted? This was too much for her to handle. All of a sudden, she felt the walls closing in around her and she needed to get out of that room for some air.

Reggie continued to talk to Sara about her parents and was about to relay information to her about other people he saw present when she started to cry. He had never seen her like this. Her face was a mess and she looked nothing like the composed, professional Sara that Reggie saw every day at work. Obviously, she was unprepared for something like this. She just sat there staring at nothing. It was starting to creep him out. His head hung and he laid back on the bed, looking up at the ceiling then at his parents. They had worried expressions on their faces, not really comprehending what was going on. This was the perfect time to explain what had happened to him during his two NDE's.

This was going to be a dandy. "Mom, Dad—there's something I need to share with you. Actually, more than one thing. You two better sit down. Pull up two chairs. This will take a while. You don't have to believe me, but at least hear me out. Please?" Reggie sincerely hoped with all his heart that his parents would not collapse like Sara did just now. He guessed she was just not the one for him if she could not trust him with anything.

"Mom, don't I have a sister?" Might as well as start out with a bang and let the cat out of the bag right away.

He could see the confusion on her face. "What do you mean? You know you are the only child! That hit and run really must have confused you. I am so sorry, honey. We better let you lay down for a bit."

There was no way he was quitting now. It was important to explain all this or he would never earn their trust from this point on.

"No, Mom! You had a miscarriage, didn't you? After I was born. When I was out of the house. You never told me anything. You told me you were going away for awhile and needed a break from Dad. When you came back, you did not seem the same as before. I was supposed to have a sister, wasn't I?"

Mom looked at Reggie and at Dad, her eyes as big as saucers. Their faces slowly turned towards him. Mom spoke first. "What?!?! How the heck did you know that? Did Dad or someone else tell you that?"

"Dad never told me anything. When I was in a coma the first time, I saw Grandma Rosie, Grandpa Joe, Grandma Sam, and Grandpa Mal. Plus, some girl ran up to me and gave me the greatest hug I'd ever gotten. She was so beautiful and had long, wavy hair just like you! She told me she was my sister Arielle and she was so happy to see me!" Reggie looked at both of his parents, hoping this would get through to them and that they would believe him.

Dad cleared his throat and was struggling to talk. Reggie forgot to let them know he was able to comprehend sign. So, he repeated what he had just uttered, but with voice off in ASL. It was difficult, but he was able to move his arms slowly. Their expressions turned into surprise. Finally, Dad was able to speak.

"Reggie! When did you get your signing back? Also, you are right about having a sister. Mom had a miscarriage when you were much younger and we never told you about it. The very fact that you know means you really did meet her. You said her name is Arielle? We were planning to name her exactly that! She must have overheard us somehow or maybe your grandparents did!" He was unable to continue, being overwhelmed with emotion.

Reggie motioned for his parents and Sara to come closer so he could wrap his arms around them. "Group hug!" It was something Reggie had done as a kid whenever he wanted to lighten up the tension in the room. But he had not done it for many years and this was a great time to do it again. They did come close to him and they hugged together. There was a lightness in the room then Dad pulled back, looking at him with a serious expression on his face.

"Son, you are telling me you can see spirits that crossed over? Like 'Long Island Medium' stuff?" He had never liked the show and neither did Mom. Reggie had watched it a few times, but never bought into it. James Randi always used to have an explanation for every so-called huckster that cold-read people or something like that. But now he was a believer, having the gift that the famous mediums had.

Mom still wasn't sold. "So you are like Whoopi Goldberg on 'Ghost' doing all that séance stuff for money?"

"No way am I going to rip people off by pretending to be something I am not! Also, I don't plan to charge a lot of money for this like many other mediums do, costing thousands of dollars each session!" Reggie slammed the bed with his right fist and immediately felt pain shoot up his arm. He flinched and grimaced. It was so obvious that they both looked at him with concern.

"I am all right, just hit the bed too hard. I really need the rest. Can I lie down and rest? It really is draining to do this like Oda Mae." Mom smiled broadly at the mention of that name, as she was the most ardent 'Ghost' fan, watching that movie countless times even though she really had doubts that anyone could talk to the dead.

All of a sudden, Reggie could see transparent figures outside his hospital room. He groaned and wondered if it would always be like this. He thought for a minute and vowed to figure out a way to zone the spirits out like Lisa Williams did when she donned her bonny cap as she drove to/from her office. She found her way of blocking out spirits when she needed privacy. Reggie knew he would need to do the same thing. All in good time. But he also knew he had quite a priceless gift and he would not squander it away. Nor would he restrict access to those who had money.

Everyone, in his opinion, deserved a reunion with loved ones who had passed on.

Plus, he had his signing back! His arms were becoming much lighter quickly. "Sara, did you see me signing again?"

She had recovered her composure by now and she smiled through her tears.

"YES, REGGIE. YOU UNDERSTAND ME NOW, TRUE-BIZ?"

Reggie laughed and nodded, as their eyes met across the bed. He thought about the first time he'd told her about TRUE-BIZ. It meant, in ASL, that it was truly 100% for real with no doubts about anything. She slowly got up off her chair and stood next to him. His left hand found her right hand and they grasped into a lock. It felt nice to have her sticking by him the whole time.

Now Dean Esfahani would have no issue with him going back to work. Sara and he could switch their roles again and he'd return to the classroom taking up his usual teaching duties. As one of his speech teachers had once told him, every cloud had a silver lining. Without Marcus Brossler, he may have never had gotten his ASL skills back. Who knows? He didn't want to think about what-ifs anymore. All he knew right now was that he was fluent in ASL again. Only if it were that easy for his students. He laughed suddenly and Sara looked at him, questioningly.

NEVER-MIND, TELL YOU LATER. he signed to her. "See? I knew I would get it all back eventually. But what I can do is take turns speaking and talking!" He saw his parents watching him and he waved an ILY at them. It was so good to be back. He felt like Dorothy at the end of "Wizard of Oz" when she exclaimed to Auntie Em that it was so good to be home.

They did have one last hurdle remaining and that was to meet with Dean Esfahani and the Board of Trustees along with the president of LVCC to keep them on top of things with the situation.

Days went by and Reggie recovered fully from passing out due to overstress. It felt like he'd escaped death twice. The following weekend, he got a video relay call from Nightline at home. Someone had heard about what happened while he was in the hospital and they wanted to do a feature story on him. It would only be ten minutes or so, but he felt honored that they wanted to spread his story to the world.

Ever since he'd watched Peter Jennings do his evening newscasts on ABC News, he'd really frequented ABC because of all the shows that were captioned back in the 1980's—Happy Days, Laverne and Shirley, Love Boat (that was the only song that he actually knew!), Fantasy Island, Eight is Enough, and the miniseries (Shogun, Roots, North and South) that he'd enjoyed as a high school student. Now ABC was calling him so he could be on that network. He was nervous and excited.

Chapter 29

Roya Esfahani was exhausted. What a few weeks it had been! All of the drama surrounding Reggie Kelleher had been too much for her. But Sara Zaslow had really saved the day with her idea of switching their jobs, only until Reggie got his ASL skills back. Their ASL classes were among the most popular at LVCC and they filled up very quickly in spite of Reggie's reputation. From what she'd heard recently, he had a "Scrooge moment" in that he became very kind, understanding, and easy to approach. If that was true, then their program would become even more popular soon once word got out.

She was still at her office and she loved being here. There was no need to go home anymore. Her two kids had flown the nest, going off to college. Her oldest, a daughter, went to Northwestern to become a lawyer. Her second child, a son, had just started his first year at Arizona State University. His major? Partying! She had warned him, though, that his grades better be good, at least 3.0, for her to continue supporting him.

There was a Subway right near school, but her meal choices were pretty limited. She could only eat halal meat, as she was a Muslim. Even though she was pretty liberal as they came, she still wanted to respect her family traditions and only eat meat that was prepared according to certain criteria. She salivated at the pepperoni pizza that people got at Subway, but that had pork. She also could use a drink of red wine, but that was alcohol and she could not imbibe any intoxicants. She could remember verbatim what her parents had told her in Iran about eating carrion and scavengers. It had been drilled into her.

She knew that had ruined her marriage with a person who was not a Muslim. While they had many things in common, the differences just had been too many. He disappeared one day and never came back. She had been unable to find him so she could have his wages garnished. It was just as well. She raised the two children alone, and worked her way up from being a professor to her current position. But it was still no piece of cake being an administrator. There were plenty of headaches and the looming budget crisis was not going to make it easier.

It was time to pray to Khuda, the Persian name for God. Her Arabic friends used the term "Allah", but it was all the same to her. Taking a rug from her closet, she spread it on the floor. Closing and locking the door to prevent anyone from bothering her, she got on her knees in the direction of Mecca and muttered the Shahada, the "Declaration of Faith".

She started her prayers with recitation. "Al-hamdu lillah" (Thanks, God) Then, she uttered, "As-salamu alaykum wa Rahmatullah." ("Peace and mercy of God be unto you.") She then looked to her right and left. Those were the angels protecting her from harm and jotting down all of the good and bad things she did every day. Not bothering to do the supplications this time, she got up after five minutes of meditation. This was good for her, to escape the outside world for a little bit.

Putting the rug back in the closet, she glanced at her bookshelves. She was a big fan of poetry and smiled at the various tomes that she proudly featured in her office. Her favorite poet was Jalal al-Din Rumi, a thirteenth century figure who had been born in Afghanistan and lived most of his life in Turkey. He was the best-selling poet in the United States and wrote in Farsi, translated into English. She also was fond of Mohja Kahif, an American Muslim woman who had written "E-mails from Schherazad" and she also read Daniel Abdul-Hayy Moore who had written poems that combined Sufi traditions and 20th century American writing.

Enough of poetry. Time to get back to brass tacks. She was not in the mood to read the stack of papers on her desk. Why not turn on the Internet and watch ABC News, her favorite network? She sat down at her desk chair and guiltily eyed the bottom right drawer, thinking of her favorite snack. Only if her parents knew what was in there! Marshmallows! Growing up, she had never had the privilege of eating them ever since second grade, when she gobbled up a handful at a Halloween party. She never forgot what happened after that.

Her father came into the classroom as she was munching the last few marshmallows and he became very upset with her. She could not figure out why until he walked her out into the hallway and gave her a lecture she would never forget.

"Roya, you cannot eat those again. Ever. You are a Muslim and you are prohibited from having anything from a pig. Marshmallows contain gelatin. The problem is gelatin can come from pigs, horses, or cows. We do not know which so we avoid anything that contains gelatin. It is spelled G-E-L-A-T-I-N. You can only have the halal version or even a vegan kind. Do you understand me? I am not angry with you, as you did not know. OK?" He looked down on her with a kindly expression just so she was not afraid or cowering.

She came back to the present, sighed and silently said, "Sorry, Dad" as she opened the drawer and took out the bag of marshmallows, eating one at a time. They were so good, weren't they? She missed Mom and Dad. They were both gone and she was alone in the world except for her colleagues. She did not have many friends and often spent the holidays alone. She did not even want to think about dating anyone ever again after she had been mistreated by her last boyfriend a few weeks ago. It had been a tumultuous relationship. What had saved her was watching "Dr. Phil" and his emphasis on avoiding abusive partners.

The computer hummed and finally she heard a ping as ABC News came online. Yawning, she sat back and closed her eyes to enjoy Diane Sawyer's melodious voice droning on about different world events. It rarely changed from day to day, as she talked about the Middle East tensions between Israel and the Palestinians, the ice-cold weather in the Northeast, and about this new deaf psychic that had already gotten 500,000 Twitter followers . . . what was that, again? Her eyes opened immediately and she perked up her ears to listen carefully.

Did she hear this correctly? Reggie Kelleher?!?!? She leaned forward, arching an eyebrow and listened even more intently to Diane Sawyer. Yes, it was Reggie. Sara sat next to him as Andrew Cuomo interviewed them both in the studio. She snatched up a legal pad and furiously looked around for a pen, finally grasping one that she saw near some books. She started scribbling as she tried to make some sense out of what she was hearing. This was just plain ridiculous! She had been more than willing to bend over backwards when Sara Zaslow came up to her about Reggie's situation, switching positions until he got all of his ASL skills back. But this was just unforgivable and would give LVCC a bad name, in her opinion.

Andrew Cuomo was saying, ". . . so you discovered the new gift, as you call it, when you woke up from passing out the other day?

I understand that Sara's ex-boyfriend had gone after both of you and some other man intervened, saving the day. Do you know who that was? No? Okay. Thank you for the opportunity to interview you and this will be on Primetime tonight for those of you who want to watch the entire segment. Back to you, Diane . . .'

In disgust, she tuned out the rest of the program and sighed. This would require a meeting with both Reggie and Sara. Rubbing her jaw, she could feel the tension setting in again that had been there many times before. Dialing Sara's number from memory, she braced herself to be absolutely noncommittal so there would be no suspicion of why she was summoning both of them to her office immediately.

"Hi, is this Sara? Yes, Roya here. How are you doing?" She purposely kept her voice light as if nothing was wrong. "Can you and Reggie come in tonight for a short meeting with me? I just need to get the latest update on what is going on with the switch in jobs. Is there anything new I need to know?"

Sara was really taken aback. A meeting now, at night? Even if it was only 6 p.m., that was quite unusual. Was something wrong? "Is everything all right with you, Roya? Okay, I will text Reggie and head over to your office. FYI, he can sign fluently again so we won't need to switch our jobs any more. Isn't that great?"

"Yes, that is fantastic! A huge relief. See you both very soon." She got up and paced around her desk. What was she going to say to them? She needed to get to the bottom of this before deciding whether to take action with the president of the college. She had a lot of power on campus and she knew she could make life difficult for the two of them if she wanted to go that route. She now wished she could sign, as that would have made things easier. Her thoughts went back to when she was young and her father had told her it was impossible for those who had passed on to speak to the living. This was an abomination in God's eyes, or so she had been told.

Before she knew it, there was a knock and she loudly said, "Come on in! Do you want any coffee or water?" It was good to see Reggie up and about, seemingly unaffected by both the car accident and the fainting incident. Then, she saw Reggie's facial expression change instantly to that of puzzlement.

Chapter 30

Oh, boy. How was Reggie going to tell the dean this one? As he entered the Dean's office, he could see someone standing right beside Roya. This man was very tall, had a thick beard, a crop of curly brown hair that looked unruly like himself, and a stare that looked like it would make anyone wilt right there and then. Then, Reggie noticed his hands. They were callused and it was obvious he had been a manual laborer while he was alive.

"Dean, I think we better sit down for this. I have something to share with you. Perhaps you saw the brief newscast about me and my new gift. I am not going to beat around the bush with you, as I have all the utmost respect for you. Now . . ." Reggie waited a few more seconds and when he saw Roya and Sara finally seated, he continued.

"I see a man beside you. He is about 50 years old, he looks very tall to me. Easily over six feet, towering. Has a really thick beard and unruly hair. Wow, his hands are enormous and it looks like he worked with them his whole life. Is this a father figure?" He paused and waited for Roya's reaction which he knew would be one of incredulity.

Sure enough, she just stopped moving and Reggie could have sworn she even stopped breathing! It just seemed like it as she stared at him, unmoving. "Reggie, you better not be conning me here!" Roya looked over to Sara. "Are you interpreting for me, please?"

Reggie could lipread what Roya had just said, but he wisely kept quiet for practical purposes. Sara signed what Roya said.

YES THIS IS MY FATHER, Sara interpreted what Roya was saying.

"He talks about Sherjangi. Something to do with poetry when you were a little girl around eight years of age?"

WOW, YES! WE HAD A GAME WITH OUR FARSI TEACHER. I WOULD RECITE A VERSE FROM ANY POEM AND THE NEXT STUDENT HAD SIXTY SECONDS TO REPLY WITH ANOTHER VERSE THAT STARTED WITH THE SAME LETTER AT THE END OF YOURS.

"You were a voracious reader, weren't you? These are pretty long names I am getting from him . . . Jalal al-Din Rumi? Never heard of him or her—Moja Kaf? I probably have that wrong . . . Hay More?" Those names were throwing me off, but I did the best I could.

"Also, he is telling me to tell you about the marshmallows and when you were young, he caught you eating them at a costume party. Does that make any sense? You weren't supposed to eat them at all. But you did not know at that time."

Roya gasped and could not believe her ears at what Reggie was saying. How in the world could he have known all this? No lucky guesses here. He had been spot-on. Was her father really standing next to her right now? She had never told anyone about her secret with the marshmallows except for her mother who was already passed on. Wait, why was her father present and not her mother? She immediately became sad because of that. But it appeared Reggie was not finished just yet.

"Roya, I am sensing that you are very sad. Here's a verse for you: 'When we are dead, seek not our tomb in the earth, but find it in the hearts of men.' Does that make any sense at all? I have never heard this quote before." Reggie looked at her intently, waiting for an answer. Roya could hardly breathe. That was Rumi's famous verse about holding loved ones in your heart, one of her absolute favorites! There was no more doubt in her mind and heart that Reggie was for real.

"Reggie, you really see my father next to me? I don't know what to say! I was going to recommend to the president that you and Sara face disciplinary action because of the newscast, but now I am not going to do anything. This is such a remarkable gift . . ." She saw that Sara was not signing anything and she stopped talking. Hopefully, Sara would get the hint and interpret again.

"I can understand everything you are saying, Dean Esfahani." Reggie smiled and there was a gleam in his eyes. Roya was taken aback and surprised to hear him say something like that. "I am fine one-on-one. That's why Sara and I were able to converse even when I had forgotten all of my signs before.

"Wait . . . your father is asking me something else. How come you aren't using your . . ." Reggie leaned forward and looked towards Roya's right side. "From what I'm understanding, a chadore . . . C-H-A-D-O-R-E. I am spelling it out loud for you so it will be evident what I am referring to. It is supposed to cover you from head to toe in white with only your face showing. How come you don't do that every time?"

Reggie playfully wagged his index finger at Roya and she just slumped back in her chair. She was now really convinced he was the real deal. Nobody knew about the rug and her not using the chadore. Nobody in the universe! Yet he had told her this vital piece of information without any effort on his part. That was really unbelievable!

She tried to think of what to say or think. That was it! Her brother, Mital, was a public relations marketer. What he would do with Reggie! He'd have a field day with offers from anyone and everyone for his services.

"Have you started thinking about getting a public relations person for your services yet, Reggie?" She was surprised he could lipread her that well and she sometimes forgot he was deaf, as Sara was not signing for her right now. She hoped that Mital could really help him, as this was the real deal. Her friends would call her the Shark Tank Dean, as she had an uncanny eye for good deals and stocks which helped her pad her 403b retirement plan at work. She was all set for life thanks to some really good stock buys over the years.

From the looks on Reggie and Sara's faces, she knew she had struck gold. They did not seem to have even registered the notion of needing someone to handle all of the phone calls and emails that would undoubtedly be coming very soon. She had better educate them, as she had learned from her brother who was a fixture in Vegas when it came to this sort of thing.

Chapter 31

Listening to Roya, Reggie had not even realized he'd needed a spokesperson for his new gift. But he realized she was right and he turned to look at Sara, giving her a questioning expression with his eyebrows up. He knew she would catch on, as it was the typical face expression for YES-NO questions, one of the things he taught his ASL 101 students at LVCC. By the end of the first semester, they would be able to differentiate between YES-NO questions and WH-questions (eyebrows furrowed). At least, that was his hope! Some still were confused after two or three months, but that was not his fault at all. He always drove the point home all semester, especially before the second test. Yet, some had gotten the two mixed up, losing valuable points in the process. There was nothing else he could have done except spoon-feed them. It was one of the most frustrating things about being an ASL professor.

Sara spoke first. "Absolutely, you do need a front person for the wave of people that will be coming to you. Remember Theresa Caputo on her show? She drowned in all of the emails and everything, so she resorted to hiring people to work for her full-time. I think it is a great idea!" She gave Roya a thumbs-up and looked back at Reggie.

He had a strong conviction that both Roya and Sara were right about this. But who to hire? "Umm . . . that's all fine, but who should I call? Ghostbusters?" He chuckled at his own joke even though it was pretty lame. Wait, Roya's father was gone! He had been standing there a minute ago, so now where was he?

"Roya, just an FYI. Your father is not here anymore, so I guess he is done with his messages. Do you know someone I can contact for public relations? Something tells me you were just thinking of someone for this purpose."

He sincerely hoped that Sara and he could tackle this next phase of his life as gracefully as some of the famous psychics had already done. They were perfect role models for him to follow. It looked like their time in her office was done. He was very relieved that there would be no loss of his job and Sara's, as it had appeared to be heading that way when they first got here today.

As if communicated telepathically, both Sara and Reggie got up at the same time and said their goodbyes to Roya. They would be hearing from Mital pretty soon and Reggie hopefully would become a famous icon of Vegas. Still, he had to go back to teaching classes and he was hoping to get a warm reception from his new 101 students.

Time went by quickly and before they knew it, they were back to teaching again. Mital did contact him and Reggie was slated to go onto the local news for a segment in a few days, after the spring semester started. He needed to prove that he was for real. Already, his appointment book was filling up quickly with word-of-mouth referrals and he steeled himself for the onslaught that would happen. But Sara and he wanted their January break first to get their second wind after everything that had happened.

Chapter 32

Finally, the first day of classes was at their doorstep. Reggie drove over to LVCC from his parents' house and did the usual, checking his mailbox which was finally empty after he'd gone through the mountain of mail and phone messages that he'd gotten after he came home from the hospital. Taking a few steps out of the office, he came to his office door. His hand fumbled in the front right pocket for the key and he opened the door to a dark office. It was like nothing had happened over the past few months. Felt good to be back, ASL skills intact, albeit with a brand-new cherished gift that would change his life.

It was now 7:50 and time to go to his first class. Reggie was one of the professors who had asked for the earliest time slots. He was a morning person. Tuesdays and Thursdays, he had a 7 a.m. slot and was the only person in his department who wanted that time. Grabbing his Signing Naturally teacher's edition and some notes, he flew out of the office (not literally) and walked briskly to the classroom where he was to have his first class of the day. Hoping this would be a nice group, he neared the door and stood there in stunned silence. What was this? A paper notice signed by Dean Esfahani saying the class had to be moved to one of the big conference rooms? Why? He walked closer to read the notice:

PROF. KELLEHER'S CLASS HAS BEEN MOVED TO SMITHSON
CONFERENCE ROOM 1. THERE IS A WATER LEAK.
PLEASE GO OVER AND ENTER FOR
ASL 101 TODAY, MONDAY.

THANK YOU FOR UNDERSTANDING,
DEAN ESFAHANI

Reggie had never seen anything like this before. Strange, he had not gotten any information about this last night. But the notice was stamped by the Dean's office with APPROVED and today's date along with Roya's signature which he recognized easily. But why conference room 1? That was a huge room with much more space than we needed for only 22 students. Sighing, he figured this was just another of LVCC's famous quirks which were legendary. The way they did business at this college made everyone's mind spin. If it were a private business, it would have gone bankrupt a long time ago.

Looking at his watch, he saw that it was 7:52 and figured he better hurry down the hall to make it to his class on time with room to spare. He liked to write the class agenda on the board along with the homework due for the next class. Plus, he enjoyed the few minutes of quiet before class began. This was not to happen today. What he saw next would really blow him away.

Chapter 33

Sara stood near the door in the darkness. She shushed everyone who was standing around the classroom. Then, she realized what she was doing. Laughing, she shook her head and whispered, "Never mind! I must be really out of it. He won't hear you all anyway." Everyone joined in the laughter, even Dean Roya Esfahani. Anyone who had been touched by Reggie's struggles was in the conference room. Even Lindsay Veniglio, who was not in ASL 101 anymore, was here along with some of her classmates and students from Reggie's other 101 sections.

She could hear his footsteps. It was funny how she could recognize the sound. As Reggie could not hear at all, he stepped very loudly wherever he went. Sara had to teach him to practically tiptoe at home whenever she was sleeping. His parents had never told him how much noise he made just walking around, slamming doors shut, flushing the toilet, and so forth. But, at LVCC, Reggie let go of that mentality and made a lot of noise. For once, she was glad he did. He was coming in a few seconds! She could not wait to see his expression when he opened the door and turned the lights on.

Reggie had just opened the door, puzzled that it was dark and nobody was here yet. He had not yet had his caffeinated coffee (in class, he explained that the word 'decaf' looked like 'deaf" when lipreading which meant 'regular' meant 'hearing') so he was operating in sort of a fog at that moment. His mind did not yet register the figures that were standing in the furthest part of the room. He flicked on the light and jumped back. What was this? Everyone was here, including Sara and his old students! Even the Dean was standing near the door to be a part of the surprise.

To show how surprised he was, Reggie put both hands on his heart and mimicked having a heart attack. "Wow!" He voiced and signed. "You guys really got me!" They sure had. Reggie had had no inkling this was coming. He looked around and his eyes misted over as he recognized all of the faces from the past semester. Looking at Sara, he playfully wagged his right index finger and shook his head in mock consternation. Then, he walked over to hug her. Acting impulsively, he stepped back and kissed her on the lips. What made him do that? He did not know, but he didn't care who saw it anymore.

Chapter 34

Lindsay Veniglio could not wait to see her favorite professor's reaction. She stood expectantly among her classmates and then jumped gleefully when Reggie pretended to have a heart attack. His eyes roved around the room and locked onto hers. He nodded at her. Then, she got the shock of her life when he kissed Sara Zaslow. They were an item! She could not believe it. Her mind scrambled to process this new information.

She was really happy for him. Keeping his job, getting his health back after such a scary time, and finding the love of his life? That was the trifecta! She smiled at him broadly as he and Sara ended their kiss. Sure enough, he walked over to Lindsay and hugged her tightly.

"Lindsay, I wanted to thank you again for being supportive at the hospital. I will never forget that. Thank you from the bottom of my heart!"

Wasn't that so nice of Reggie? His voice was interesting. She could tell he was deaf from listening to him. It was more of a robotic voice, lacking the nuances of intonation that hearing people learned to use on a daily basis. But she could understand every word he said and for a profoundly deaf person, he spoke very clearly. She would not mind being with a deaf man. Maybe one day she would find her own Reggie! Armed with that conviction in her mind, she vowed to find her own deaf guy someday.

Roya also was surprised when Sara and Reggie kissed. But there was nothing in the contract forbidding office romances. While Sara was technically the ASL supervisor, it was not an official position. She was merely the lab coordinator and he was just a colleague of hers. If she had been the chairperson of the whole department, that might have caused ripples and eventually problems would have ensued. But this was all kosher. She chuckled at even the thought. She should have been thinking, 'This was all halal'!

She wanted to propose a toast to Reggie, one of the bravest people she had ever known. She looked at the long table in the middle of the room. There was, of course, no alcohol as this was a college. But a soda would be just fine. In the midst of all the hugging and shaking hands around her, she poured Diet Coke into a plastic glass and lifted it up for all to see. As she had a huge presence on campus, everyone who was around her quieted immediately.

In a few seconds, all eyes were upon her. "Reggie . . . Sara, can you interpret for me? Thank you . . ." She paused for a second to gather her thoughts on what to say for this occasion, one that very few people ever thought would take place as everyone had thought Reggie would not recover from his injuries.

"You are a brave soul with your willingness to overcome injuries and trauma to return to our campus . . ." She could hear many people yelling, "Hear, hear!" She was surprised to see hands waving in the air.

She looked at Reggie intently and smiled. Their encounter in her office had really shaken the core of her foundations and changed her outlook on life itself. It had been that profound. She owed him an amount of gratitude that she would never be able to repay in her lifetime.

"We are happy you are back with us at LVCC and we look forward to many more years of you being here, teaching with your usual excellence and enthusiasm!" She figured that was enough and ended her toast with: "Here's to you, Professor Kelleher! Hear, hear! Speech!"

Reggie was stunned. Was that Roya giving him a toast? Now he'd seen everything. She was so reticent, like a granite of stone, whenever she was on campus. Everyone was staring at her and Reggie wouldn't be surprised if they thought aliens had snatched her and replaced her with some doppelganger from their own planet. It was a widespread joke that Dean Esfahani was their own version of Spock, with no emotion. But there she was, smiling as she toasted him. Sara signed what Roya uttered out loud and it was so nice being able to understand ASL easily again.

As the Dean finished her toast and yelled for a speech, all eyes turned to him. Should he sign or speak now? Remembering the controversy surrounding Marlee Matlin's acceptance speech as she received her Oscar back in the 1980's, he decided to go ahead and use ASL. His eyes searched out Sara and she walked over to him again, putting her right arm around his waist. It felt good to be standing with her, not just alongside her. Today was the day they went public, thanks to his public display of affection.

He started signing and could see in his peripheral vision that Sara was voicing for him. What would he have done without her? Happily, he would not have to find out.

"Thank you for coming this morning . . ." He was at a loss for words for a change. "This was absolutely, totally unexpected. I was just walking to the classroom and when I saw that notice, I was not sure what to think. It had not rained for the past few days and I did not suspect a thing! I really appreciate the show of support. I hate to put a damper on things, but it's time to get back to the business of ASL!"

Groans and sighs were evident all around the room, but it was all good natured. Reggie shrugged his shoulders and hugged Sara again. This was going to be a new Reggie Kelleher teaching. No more "God in the Classroom" syndrome. He was going to be kind, patient, funny, and everything else he should have been in the past. He looked at everyone and waved. He took the time to approach every person who had showed up for this small party.

He expressed his appreciation and noticed the pleased reaction of each student and faculty member there while he did that. Then, he walked out of the conference room to go back to the classroom. It was going to be a great semester! He had much to look forward to and would see his parents later to celebrate out at a restaurant with Sara.

As Reggie exited the conference room, he paused and turned around to look at everyone one more time. He stopped all of a sudden, standing at the doorway. A thought came to his mind. Remembering the gaggle of students exchanging five-dollar bills the previous semester, making a certain bet, Reggie decided to make someone happy. He made sure all eyes were upon him right there and then.

He looked at every face that was in the room, one by one. Once he had looked at everyone, his eyes were twinkling as he smiled the broadest, biggest, most radiant smile he had ever had.

Then, even he heard someone yelling and could see her jumping up and down, waving her hands in the air in glee. That one ASL student just became rich at that moment, as he had finally smiled in public, especially in front of ASL students. She had won the "When Will Rego Smile?" betting pool. Some students had even put money in that he would never smile in public until after their graduation. But Sara had led him to a better life. He became much more vibrant, happy, and relaxed. People could not believe the transformation. This was his rebirth! Rebirth of Signs.